Facing the Enemy

A Caroline Classic
Volume 2

by Kathleen Ernst

⭐ AmericanGirl®

Published by American Girl Publishing
Copyright © 2014 American Girl

Questions or comments? Call 1-800-845-0005,
visit **americangirl.com**, or write to Customer Service,
American Girl, 8400 Fairway Place, Middleton, WI 53562.

Printed in China
14 15 16 17 18 19 20 LEO 10 9 8 7 6 5 4 3 2 1

All American Girl marks, Beforever™, Caroline™,
and Caroline Abbott™ are trademarks of American Girl.

This book is a work of fiction. Any similarity to real persons, living or dead,
is coincidental and not intended by American Girl. References to real events,
people, or places are used fictitiously. Other names, characters, places, and
incidents are the products of imagination.

Cover image by Michael Dwornik and Juliana Kolesova

Cataloging-in-Publication Data available from the Library of Congress

*For Scott and Meghan,
for their faith and support*

*For Constance Barone, Dianne Graves,
James Spurr, and Stephan Wallace;
and for everyone who has worked to
preserve and interpret Sackets Harbor's
rich heritage, with thanks*

*And for my friends at American Girl,
past and present, who have helped
make each book the best it can be*

Beforever

Beforever is about making connections.
It's about exploring the past, finding your
place in the present, and thinking about the
possibilities your future can bring. And it's about
seeing the common thread that ties girls from
all times together. The inspiring characters you
will meet stand up for what they care about
most: Helping others. Protecting the earth.
Overcoming injustice. Through their courageous
stories, discover how staying true to your own
beliefs will help make your world better
today—and tomorrow.

≳ TABLE *of* CONTENTS ≲

A Spring Adventure

≈CHAPTER 1≈

May 1813

aroline Abbott smiled as she walked down the hill in the little village of Sackets Harbor, New York. *Finally,* a soft spring day had arrived! The winter had been long and icy, and then hard rains had pelted the countryside. Today, though, May sunshine sparkled on the blue-green waters of Lake Ontario.

Soon the "Abbott's" sign that hung above her family's shipyard came into view. Caroline's mother had been in charge of the shipyard for almost a year now—ever since war had broken out and Papa had been captured by the British. Caroline missed Papa terribly. She was also very proud of Mama, who had kept the business going.

Caroline shielded her eyes with her hand and squinted over the water. Almost all travel to and from

Sackets Harbor involved ships on Lake Ontario. Now that the winter's ice had melted, the first supply boats of the year would arrive any day. That would be something to celebrate!

Caroline was concentrating so hard that she didn't see Hosea Barton, the sailmaker, until he walked from the yard. "Good morning, miss," he said. "See any boats out there?"

"Not yet," Caroline sighed. "I was hoping to see Irish Jack's boat. He promised Mama last fall that he'd bring supplies for the shipyard as soon as the ice melted. And *I* am waiting to see what new colors of embroidery silk he brings!" Irish Jack was a family friend, and he never failed to tuck a few sewing supplies for Caroline in with his other cargo.

"I hope he comes soon," Hosea said. He sounded more worried than excited.

Caroline looked at her friend. "Is something wrong?"

"We're completely out of sailcloth," Hosea told her. "I have nothing left to work with."

Caroline stared at him with dismay. She hadn't realized how badly the supply boats were needed.

"Did Mr. Tate send you home?" she asked anxiously. Mr. Tate was the chief carpenter.

"No, child," Hosea assured her. "I'm running an errand for him. Mr. Tate is trying to keep me busy. We're all waiting to see Irish Jack's boat, though. We're desperate for the supplies he's carrying." Hosea tipped his hat and continued on his way.

Caroline walked slowly into the shipyard. Since war had been declared, the workers had been busy making gunboats for the American navy. It was usually a treat to spend time here—Caroline liked watching the men turn pieces of wood and bits of iron into huge ships. Now, though, the spring afternoon no longer seemed quite as sweet.

In the shipyard, Caroline saw Mr. Tate talking to Mama. "I'm sorry, Mrs. Abbott," he was saying, "but if those supplies don't come in the next few days, we'll have to close the yard. We need bolts, nails, tar, paint . . . without them, we can't work."

"Let's pray our supply boat arrives, then," Mama told him. "We have to finish that gunboat."

Mama went into the office and closed the door behind her. As Caroline watched Mr. Tate walk away, she thought about what she'd heard. Her chest suddenly felt fluttery inside as a new worry struck her. *The supply boat being late is bad enough,* she thought. *But what if Irish Jack doesn't arrive at all?* Caroline knew that British ships were always prowling Lake Ontario, looking for American boats to capture or sink. Now she realized that Irish Jack's boat would be a special prize. An enemy captain could take Jack and his men prisoner—and deliver all those supplies to the British across the lake in Upper Canada!

Caroline tiptoed closer to the office and peeked in the window. Mama sat on the stool in front of Papa's desk, her face in her hands. Caroline knocked on the door, then opened it. "Mama?" she called. "It's me."

Mama sat up straight, looking startled. "Oh! Caroline, I—I didn't know you were coming today." She picked up a stack of papers and tapped the edges on the desk to straighten them.

"Grandmother said I might," Caroline explained.

Mama nodded. But she looked as if her mind was somewhere else.

"I heard you talking with Mr. Tate," Caroline

said. "And Hosea told me that he's used the last of the sailcloth. Could you borrow some supplies from the navy shipyard?"

"I asked." Mama shook her head. "The navy ship-builders have nothing to spare for us. *Everyone* is waiting for the supply boats. The soldiers and sailors are even running low on food! The supply boats will bring them barrels of salt pork and bags of pilot bread." She sighed. "At least we have our garden. Still, if Irish Jack doesn't come soon, our shipyard will be in trouble."

Caroline swallowed hard as she imagined Irish Jack's dangerous trip to Sackets Harbor. "Do you think the British might have captured his boat?"

"It's possible," Mama admitted. "But perhaps he's just been delayed by bad weather. All we can do is wait."

Caroline nodded, but Mama's answer didn't make her feel any better. Since the war began, she sometimes felt as if she spent all her time waiting. Waiting for news. Waiting for the supply ships. And most of all, waiting for Papa to come home. Waiting could be so *hard*.

"Let's get to work," Mama said. "I've written a

letter, but before I post it I'd like you to make a copy for our records. It will be good penmanship practice for you."

Caroline worked with Mama for the rest of the afternoon. After copying the letter, she dusted Papa's books. Keeping busy didn't chase the worries from her mind, though.

As Caroline left the office, she took a hard look around the shipyard. The war had brought Abbott's more business than ever. Caroline watched several carpenters checking measurements on the gunboat they were building. She smelled pine pitch and tar, fresh paint and varnish. The yard rang with saws whining, mallets pounding, men whistling. Caroline couldn't bear the thought of Abbott's Shipyard going still and silent. The American navy needed that gunboat to fight the British!

Caroline trudged home with her head bent. As she approached her house, she saw her good friend Rhonda Hathaway standing by the gate. Rhonda, her little sister Amelia, and Mrs. Hathaway had been lodging in Caroline's house for months.

"Did you hear anything about the American

fighters?" Rhonda called. Almost two thousand sailors and soldiers had recently sailed from Sackets Harbor, hoping to capture forts on the Canadian side of the lake. Rhonda's father, a United States Army officer, had left with them.

"There's no news," Caroline told her friend sympathetically.

"I came outside hoping I might see my father walking down the lane," Rhonda said. "I know it's silly of me to watch for him, but—"

"It's *not* silly," Caroline assured her. "I know exactly how you feel."

Rhonda grabbed Caroline's hand. "Your papa has been gone such a long time! I don't know how you bear it."

Caroline felt the Papa-place in her heart squeeze tight. She gazed in the direction of the British stronghold of Kingston in Upper Canada. The last time she'd seen Papa, he was a prisoner there. When news came last fall that American prisoners might soon be sent far away, Caroline and Mama had made a dangerous trip across Lake Ontario to see him. It was the last time Caroline had seen her father.

Now, seven months later, the ache in her heart had not lessened. Was Papa still alive? Was he huddled in some cold prison? Had he managed to escape? There was no way of knowing.

"I miss him every day," Caroline said finally. "Let's go inside now, all right?"

"You go," Rhonda said. "I'm going to stay out here just a little longer."

After supper that evening, Caroline sat in the parlor with Mama, Grandmother, and the Hathaways. Each of them had some needlework project—even little Amelia, who was stitching her first sampler. Caroline was mending a torn seam in her work apron.

Usually their evenings were filled with conversation, but tonight everyone was quiet. Rhonda sighed loudly and dropped the lace that she was making into her lap. Mrs. Hathaway gave Rhonda a worried look. Then Caroline noticed that Mama's hands had stilled on her knitting, too. Mama was staring into the fire, lost in thought. Only Grandmother, who was hemming a new petticoat, seemed focused and steady.

Caroline hated all the sadness and worry. Grandmother always said to look for ways to help a situation instead of brooding about things that couldn't be changed. *I can't do anything about Irish Jack's supply boat,* Caroline thought, *but I can try to cheer up Rhonda.*

She sat for a moment, considering ideas. Then she smiled. "I would like to go fishing one day soon," she said, breaking the silence. "I can take the skiff."

Everyone looked startled. Mama said, "I don't have time to leave the shipyard, Caroline. And you can't go by yourself."

"No, but Seth should pay us a visit any day now," Caroline reminded her. "He's a good sailor, and he told me last time he was here that he'd been dreaming all winter about getting out on the water with a fishing pole." Her friend Seth Whittleslee was the local post walker, tramping many miles to deliver mail and newspapers to isolated farms and settlements. He was a few years older than Caroline, and a good companion on adventures.

Mama nodded. "Very well, then. If Seth can spare the time, you may go."

Caroline looked at Rhonda. "Will you come with us?"

"Me?" Rhonda blinked. "I don't know how to catch fish."

"Then it's time to learn!" Caroline told her. "Please?" She turned to Mrs. Hathaway. "With your permission."

Mrs. Hathaway looked at Mama. "Are you sure the girls will be safe?"

Mama nodded. "Seth and Caroline know how to handle the skiff."

"Then I think you should go, Rhonda," declared Mrs. Hathaway. "An outing will do you good."

Rhonda still looked uncertain, but she nodded. "All right."

"You'll have fun," Caroline promised.

As everyone settled back to their needlework, Grandmother gave Caroline an approving nod. Caroline smiled, pleased by the silent praise. She had suggested the fishing trip in hopes of helping Rhonda forget her worries for a little while. Now she discovered that *she* felt better, too!

❁

Two days later, Caroline and Rhonda walked to Abbott's Shipyard. They'd made arrangements to meet Seth at the yard for their fishing trip. No supply boat had arrived yet, and Caroline could tell that work on the gunboat was slowing to a halt. The spring weather was still beautiful, though, and she was determined to enjoy it. She could hardly wait to get out on the water!

"Today," Caroline announced, "is going to be a good day." She grabbed Rhonda's hand and swung it back and forth.

Rhonda's eyes sparkled with excitement, but she tightened her grip on Caroline's hand. "I'm a little nervous about going out in such a small boat," Rhonda admitted.

"Don't worry. Papa built the skiff," Caroline told her proudly. "*Sparrow* is the finest little skiff on Lake Ontario. And we'll stay close to shore."

Seth strolled up to them, carrying a small ax, fishing poles, and a tin pail holding worms. "Ready?" he asked.

Rhonda frowned. "You cut only two poles!"

Seth gestured to the ax. "I can easily cut another. I wasn't sure if you actually wanted to fish."

"I intend to fish," Rhonda informed him.

Caroline grinned. "Well, I intend to catch the biggest fish."

"*I* might catch the biggest fish!" Rhonda protested.

"Even if we don't catch anything, it'll be grand to be on the water," Seth said. He glanced at the unfinished gunboat. "The only thing better than taking out the skiff would be serving on a U.S. Navy ship! I hope we defeat the British for good this year."

"I do too," Caroline agreed. Then she pointed to the shed where Papa's skiff had waited out the winter. "Look! The men are bringing out *Sparrow*."

Caroline, Seth, and Rhonda hurried over. Seeing the skiff made Caroline's spirits rise even higher. The boat had sharply pointed ends and a flat bottom and was just big enough for three people. The trim had recently been repainted in crisp white, with the word *Sparrow* in blue on both sides.

Mr. Tate joined them to watch workers carry the skiff down to the dock. "She's a first-rate little boat," he said. "How your father loved to go fishing, Caroline! Especially when you went with him."

Caroline smiled, recalling happy times with Papa.

Together they had often sailed *Sparrow* to Papa's favorite fishing spot, a marshy cove called Mallard Bay. He'd built a little lean-to of tree branches for shelter there, and a fire pit. Once, he'd landed a thirty-pound trout!

"I'll take good care of the skiff," Caroline promised.

Mr. Tate squeezed her shoulder. Then he turned to the men easing the skiff into the water beside the dock. "Have a care, now! We can't have Mr. Abbott finding any scrapes on *Sparrow* when he gets home."

Seth climbed down the ladder to the skiff and tucked his gear away. Rhonda went next, clutching her skirt so that she wouldn't trip. Seth settled her in the rear seat. Then Caroline scampered to her own place in the front.

Seth set the oars carefully into their locks and began rowing. Soon they left the sheltered bay. Once they reached the great lake, the chop of the waves grew stronger, but Seth guided the skiff smoothly along the wooded shoreline. Sunlight glistened on the water, and a fresh breeze ruffled Caroline's hair.

"It's a fine day for an adventure," Rhonda said.

Caroline liked Rhonda's spirit. "If the wind stays fair, we'll be able to run up the sail soon," Caroline said. She was eager to raise the sail. She loved to pretend that she was captain of her own ship!

Seth took another pull on the oars. His long legs were better suited for his job as post walker than for sailing the skiff—sitting on the low seat forced his knees almost to his chin!

"I'm glad you could come with us," Caroline told him.

"My pleasure," he said. "What do you think, Caroline? Should we head for Mallard Bay?"

"No!" The word burst out before Caroline could stop herself. She didn't want to take the others to Papa's fish camp without him. "I mean . . . Mallard Bay is too far for Rhonda's first trip."

"There are plenty of good spots closer to home," Seth agreed. He paused for a moment, water dripping from the oars. "I'm dreaming of fresh lake trout, fried up in butter."

"Grandmother's expecting a whole string of trout," Caroline told him. She turned and scanned the lake ahead. "Oh, careful—watch out for that fallen log, Seth."

Seth began to row again. Caroline leaned to one

side carefully, using her weight to help Seth navigate around the log, just as Papa had shown her.

I'm grateful for all you taught me, Papa, she thought. She stroked *Sparrow*'s hull, knowing that Papa's hands had shaped each piece of wood.

"Well, where *shall* we go?" Rhonda asked. "I want to catch some fish!"

"How about the mouth of Hickory Creek?" Seth suggested.

Caroline grinned. The place where Hickory Creek flowed into Lake Ontario was one of her favorite fishing spots, and it wasn't too far away. "Perfect!" she said. "Let's head toward Hickory Creek."

A Desperate Race

A s the skiff traveled farther along the lakeshore, Caroline watched for familiar landmarks. "There!" she announced. "See that marshy area ahead, Rhonda?" She pointed to a swampy cove where tall grasses and cattails pushed from the water. The shoreline was wooded, with no houses in sight. "That's where Hickory Creek flows into the lake."

Seth began expertly rowing through the grasses. Several ducks launched into the air, scolding Caroline and her friends with noisy *quack-quack-quacks* as they flew away.

"Why is this a good fishing spot?" Rhonda asked.

"Two reasons," Caroline told her. "First, fish like the warmer water flowing from the creek."

"And in just a moment, you'll see the second

reason we like this spot," Seth promised.

The skiff swished through clumps of cattails. Caroline reached out to touch the leaves as they passed. She liked the way they felt in her fingers, smooth and firm. Then the skiff gently came to a stop. Beneath them, the hull made a soft scraping sound.

Rhonda looked alarmed. "Have we run aground?"

"We're on a sandbar," Caroline explained. "Look into the water. See?" The skiff rested on a long mound of sand and gravel just underwater. "It's an easy place for us to stop and fish."

"The sandbar almost blocks Hickory Creek as it flows into the marsh and on into the lake," Seth added. "There's one deeper channel that cuts through the sandbar." He pointed to an area near the far shore where the water was dark as it poured through the channel.

"Remember when we waded on the sandbar last summer?" Caroline asked Seth. He laughed, and Caroline told Rhonda how she and Seth had splashed water at each other.

"We both got soaked!" Seth said. "It makes me cold to think about it."

"But don't worry, Rhonda," Caroline added quickly. "We'll stay dry today."

"Will it take long to catch a fish?" Rhonda asked.

"Not if we're lucky!" Caroline said cheerfully. She felt lucky today. The sun was shining, the air felt warm, and she and her friends were on a fishing trip!

Seth handed each of the girls a fishing pole. A string dangled from each pole, with a wire hook on the end. Then he reached for the tin pail that held the worms.

Rhonda's nose wrinkled. "Will I have to put a worm on the hook myself?"

"Only if you want to be allowed to eat whatever you catch," Caroline teased.

"I'll do the worm for you," Seth told Rhonda.

When he had finished, Caroline showed Rhonda how to cast the hook into the water. "And now, wait until you feel a tug on the line," she explained. "That's how you know you have a fish."

"I hope I catch—" Rhonda stopped suddenly. "Oh, look!" She pointed at a long, low boat that had just come into view. An American flag fluttered from the bateau's single mast. The boat was traveling near the shore, heading toward Sackets Harbor. Rhonda's eyes lit up. "Maybe the American soldiers are returning!"

Seth shook his head. "I don't think so. Since it's by itself, it's most likely a supply boat."

Caroline's hopes soared like a gull. She held her breath, squinting at the bateau until she was able to pick out the red banner flying below the national flag. "It's Irish Jack!" she cried.

"Hurrah!" Rhonda cheered.

"Jack and his men will easily make Sackets Harbor with plenty of time to unload yet today," Seth said. "Watch out, Rhonda, I think your line got tangled in those cattails . . ." His voice trailed away. "Oh no," he whispered. He pointed straight north, past the marsh to Lake Ontario's open water.

Caroline's heart dropped as she followed his gaze. A sloop had just appeared, and she could see a British flag flying from its tallest mast. "It's an enemy ship," she whispered.

Rhonda's eyes were wide. "It's making straight for us!"

"It's not making straight for *us*," Seth said grimly. "It's making straight for the bateau."

Her heart racing, Caroline eyed the sloop. Seth was

right. Although the British sloop was zigzagging to make best use of the wind, its captain was clearly heading toward the American supply boat.

Irish Jack must have seen the enemy sloop, too. His bateau was moving quickly now. It had drawn so close to the marsh that Caroline could see Irish Jack's wild red hair. His crewmen were pulling hard at the oars.

Caroline clenched handfuls of skirt fabric in her fists. "Faster!" she urged the crew.

"Are they trying to run for Sackets Harbor?" Rhonda asked. "Why don't they raise their sail?"

"The wind's against them," Caroline told her. She felt hot inside. "All they can do is row."

"Those blasted British!" Seth said angrily. "I wish I could drive them back to Upper Canada myself!"

Caroline felt the same way. "At least the bateau is close enough to shore that the men can jump off and slip away into the woods. They won't be taken prisoner." That thought gave her a scrap of comfort, but she hated to think of the British capturing the bateau and its precious supplies.

Rhonda squinted. "They don't look as if they're planning to abandon the bateau."

"You're right," Caroline agreed. She frowned in confusion. The Americans were still rowing furiously. The bateau moved along at a good pace. What was Irish Jack doing? Now the bateau was turning, hugging the curving shore toward the marsh. Wouldn't Irish Jack make better time to Sackets Harbor if he kept his boat going in a straight line instead of turning into the marsh?

Suddenly, she understood. "He's heading for the creek!"

Seth leaned forward, watching intently. "Of *course*! That's just what I'd do. Irish Jack grew up nearby. He knows every waterway for miles around."

Rhonda pushed her bonnet back in order to see better. "Isn't the bateau too big to travel up the creek?"

"A bateau rides high in the water," Seth explained. "It will glide right through that deep channel. But if the British try to follow, they'll risk running their sloop aground on the sandbar. I'd guess Irish Jack could make it maybe half a mile or more before the creek gets too narrow and shallow for them to continue. They'll be safe from the sloop's cannons, anyway."

The British ship was well away but still making

its determined progress toward them. *"Go!"* Caroline yelled across the water to Irish Jack and his men. "You can make it!" She hugged her arms across her chest, every muscle tight, wishing she could help them row. The bateau was so close now that she could hear the oars splashing. The men were grunting with effort, bending forward and leaning back in rhythm as they strained to outrun the sloop.

As Irish Jack muscled his bateau perfectly among the cattails and on through the narrow channel, Caroline and her friends cheered. The big man gave them a quick wave before his boat slid into Hickory Creek. Soon the bateau moved around a bend and out of sight.

Caroline turned toward the British sloop. "You've lost!" she crowed, although the sailors were too far away to hear. "Turn back!"

But the sloop did not turn back. Caroline's sense of triumph turned to alarm.

"I don't believe it." Seth pounded one fist against his knee. "The captain is going to try to follow Jack!"

"I thought you said his sloop would run aground if he tried to sail into the creek," Rhonda said.

Seth narrowed his eyes, considering. "Normally it would. But the creek is running high from the spring rains. Maybe the captain thinks his sloop *could* make it through the channel. And—"

Rhonda finished the sentence. "And if it does, the British will catch the bateau."

Caroline couldn't bear to see the British seize the supplies that were so desperately needed at the shipyard. But what could she and Seth and Rhonda do? Throw their fishing poles at the sloop? Seth could hardly use his little ax to attack a British sloop armed with cannons!

Caroline closed her eyes, trying to concentrate. *All we need is one idea,* she thought. *Just one good idea . . .*

A gull called harshly. Caroline opened her eyes and saw a lone white gull dive nearby. It startled a turtle that had been sunning itself on a fallen log. Caroline stared at the log and caught her breath. Quickly, she began pulling off her shoes and stockings. "Seth!" she cried. "See that fallen log? We might be able to block the channel with it!"

Seth glanced at the log and yanked off his shoes. "It's a grand idea," he said, "although I don't know if it will work."

"We can *try*," Caroline said stubbornly. "Rhonda, lean to the far side."

Rhonda looked puzzled, but she did as Caroline asked. Caroline swung her legs over the skiff's side and slid onto the sandbar. She yelped as icy water clutched her feet, her shins, her knees. The creek water *was* higher than usual. She could feel the current tugging at her as it flowed over the sandbar.

Seth splashed down beside her. He pulled *Sparrow* higher on the sandbar, making sure it was wedged tight and wouldn't float away.

"Just sit still and you'll be fine," he told Rhonda. "Caroline, I'll haul that log over. You grab any branches you can find."

"I want to help, too!" Rhonda pulled off her shoes and stockings. Seth took her hand as she scrambled into the water.

Rhonda gasped. "Ooh—it's freezing!" Her beautiful skirt billowed like a flower before becoming water-logged. "I'll look for branches," she said.

"Be sure to stay on the sandbar, where the water isn't too deep," Caroline warned her.

The girls headed toward shore, struggling to move

through the cold water. Caroline wished she were
as tall as Seth and not wearing long skirts. The sand
shifted beneath her feet with every step. "Let's grab
that one," she said, pointing to a large branch onshore.
The girls retrieved the branch and pulled it over the
sandbar to the deep channel.

Seth waded to the log where the turtle had been
sunning. With a mighty heave, he managed to tug
it free. Caroline held her breath as he floated it back
through the cattails.

"Is it long enough to block the channel?"
Rhonda asked anxiously as Seth joined them on
the sandbar.

"We'll see." Seth pointed the log directly across
the channel and shoved it into the water.

The fast-flowing water pushed the log as if it
were a matchstick. Instead of sinking straight across
the channel, like a closed gate, the log was pushed
sideways by the current so that it sank at an angle—
like an open gate. Caroline's hopes sank like the log.

"It's a start," Seth said grimly, "but we'll need a lot
more than that log to block the channel."

Caroline quickly passed him the big branch that

she and Rhonda had found. "Try adding this!"

Seth pointed the branch and threw it into the channel like a spear, just upstream of the log. The water pushed it against the log. For a moment Caroline was afraid the branch would float away, but it settled underwater. Caroline heaved a sigh of relief. Every stick or branch that got caught against the log would help block the sloop.

"I see another one!" Rhonda called. She and Caroline splashed across the sandbar again, grabbed another dead branch, and pulled it back. Seth added a few more, trying to create a logjam of sticks.

"Will it be enough?" Caroline asked urgently.

"I don't know." Seth shook his head as the rushing creek pushed one of the dead branches free. "The water is higher than I've ever seen it."

Caroline looked over her shoulder. Her heart felt as icy as her toes. The British sloop was so close now that she could make out the figures onboard. "Can you use your ax to chop down a small tree?"

Seth shot a glance at the sloop. "We don't have enough time."

"Do you see anything else we can dump in the

channel?" Caroline cried. The three of them scanned the shore.

"There's nothing." Seth clenched his fists. "I think we have to give up."

Give up. Those two words made Caroline so angry that she could almost taste something bitter on her tongue. "No!" she said. "We *can't* let the British get the bateau. Mama needs the supplies, and Irish Jack is probably hauling things for the navy yard, too." Feeling desperate, she looked around for something, *anything*, that they could use to block the channel.

Her gaze landed on the skiff. Suddenly she realized that they did *not* have to give up, not quite yet. Tears blurred her vision, but she blinked them away. "I have one more idea," she told her friends. "We can sink *Sparrow.*"

"Caroline, no," Seth protested. Rhonda's eyes went wide.

"We must!" Caroline said fiercely. "If we don't block that channel completely, the sloop might still be able to sail through. We can use the ax to chop a hole in the hull." A single layer of planks formed the skiff's sides and bottom. It would be easy for Seth to break through—and then water would flood into the skiff and sink it.

Caroline began wading through the icy water toward the skiff. Seth and Rhonda splashed after her. When they reached it, Seth grabbed their shoes from the bottom of the skiff, stuffed their stockings inside, and hurled them to dry land.

"We need to tow the skiff to the channel," Caroline said.

Seth snatched the bowline. Rhonda and Caroline grabbed the skiff, one on each side, panting as they struggled to pull it to the channel. *Sparrow* was heavier than Caroline had expected, and their progress was slow. The enemy sloop was gaining on them.

"Quick, Seth, get the ax!" Caroline cried.

An angry shout rang across the water. It sounded close. Caroline didn't dare to glance back at the British sloop.

Seth grasped his ax. "Hold her steady! Don't let the current push her away."

The girls struggled to hold the skiff in place over the deep channel, but the current from Hickory Creek was strong. Caroline knew her aching arms couldn't hold the skiff against the rushing water. "Throw me the bowline!" she shouted to Seth.

Caroline caught the rope Seth tossed to her and reached for the end of the log he'd sunk in the channel. It had come to rest just underwater, and she needed to tie the skiff to it. She could barely see what she was doing through the tumbling water. Her numb fingers felt wooden.

"I can't hold on much longer," Rhonda whimpered.

Caroline tried to remember how to tie a strong knot. Thoughts raced through her mind so fast that she couldn't catch a single one. Panic bubbled up inside. Then she heard Papa's voice in her memory: *Sailors practice their knots so often that when they need to make one quickly, their hands remember how.*

Caroline took a deep breath and tried again. She found that her hands did indeed remember how. Soon the skiff was secured against the log. Caroline knew it would hold long enough for Seth to do his job.

Seth raised his ax. *Whack! Whack! Whack!* The blade made a horrid sound as it bit into *Sparrow*'s hull. A ragged hole opened. Water poured through. As the skiff slowly filled with water, it began to sink into the channel.

Caroline held her breath. If the current pushed the skiff free of the channel, the British might still slip through and capture the bateau—and its precious supplies.

But the heavy skiff did not float away. It stood almost on end as it sank into the channel, lodged against the log and branches already in place. The front end of the skiff settled on the sandy bottom. The back, with the word *Sparrow* gleaming in the sunlight, came to rest just above the waterline. The skiff held firm, blocking the channel.

"Will *that* keep the British from sailing through?" Rhonda asked. She was shivering.

"It must!" Caroline said. She had sacrificed her family's skiff. She couldn't bear to think that it might not save the supply boat.

Seth's chest heaved from his efforts as he scrambled up on the sandbar. "That captain would be a fool to try chasing Irish Jack now," he said.

"Be on your way," Rhonda told the British captain. She shaded her eyes with one hand, peering intently at the sloop.

Caroline imagined the British officers watching

through spyglasses as they tried to decide what to do. The next few moments seemed to pass very, *very* slowly.

Finally the sound of shouted commands drifted across the water. The crewmen adjusted the sails. The sloop turned back toward Upper Canada.

"They're giving up!" Rhonda cried. Seth whooped with joy.

Caroline could hardly believe her eyes—but there was the British sloop, sailing away in defeat. "We did it," she said. "We really did it!"

Seth's Decision

≥ CHAPTER 3 ≤

C aroline, Rhonda, and Seth sat shivering on the shore, putting on their dry stockings and shoes. They had watched the sloop until it sailed out of sight.

"How are we going to get home?" Rhonda asked.

"We'll have to walk," Seth said.

Now that the first flush of excitement was past, Caroline felt tired all the way to her bones. How far were they from Sackets Harbor?

She jumped as some branches rustled nearby. Then Irish Jack appeared through the trees. A huge grin split his face. "You three are the heroes of the day!" he called. "I got my bateau upstream as far as I could. Then I came ashore and walked back to see what the British would do. I saw how you blocked the channel. That was quick thinking!" He grabbed his hat and slapped it against his leg with delight.

Caroline scrambled to her feet. "It's good to see you," she told him. "Mama and Mr. Tate need those supplies you're carrying. We've been waiting and *waiting*."

Irish Jack shook his head. "We've had a slow trip. British captains have been sailing back and forth, ready to pounce on any American boat they can find. I've had to hide my bateau several times before this."

"You're sure the bateau is safe now?" Caroline asked.

Irish Jack ran a hand through his wild red hair, looking pleased. "Sure as the sun will rise tomorrow. My crew is guarding her. When we're certain that blasted British sloop isn't prowling about, we'll slip on to Sackets Harbor."

"But the channel is blocked now!" Rhonda said. "How will you get out?"

"Oh, we can pass through," Irish Jack promised. "Even loaded, we can pull the bateau right over the sandbar."

"That's g-good," said Rhonda. Her teeth were chattering.

"I've got blankets on my boat," Irish Jack said. "Let's go fetch them. Once you've warmed up a bit, I'll escort you home." He turned and walked back in the direction he'd come, upstream where the bateau was hidden. Seth and Rhonda followed.

Caroline started to bring up the rear, but she paused to take one last look at the channel. She could see the back end of the skiff where it had come to rest, with the word *Sparrow* above the flowing water.

Caroline swallowed hard. Papa had built that skiff! It had taken her and Papa on many happy fishing trips. It had safely gotten her and Mama all the way to Kingston and back last fall. Now she would never skim over the water in it again.

I lost my ship, Caroline thought. Papa always said that a captain who lost his ship was disgraced. What would he think of her now? Caroline's heart seemed to freeze in her chest. She felt mixed up inside—proud and ashamed, happy and sad, all at the same time.

"Caroline?" Rhonda called.

"I'm coming," Caroline answered. She took one last look at the precious skiff. Finally, she forced herself to look away.

Caroline plodded after Irish Jack as he walked her, Rhonda, and Seth home. The bateau captain did not accept Grandmother's offer to come inside for warm gingerbread. "I need to get back to my crew," he said. "But I hope you'll give these three heroes extra helpings. They did a fine thing today."

A fine thing, Caroline thought, *and a terrible thing, too.*

Once Rhonda's mother heard the story, she hurried off to fetch Mama. Grandmother found a pair of old trousers and a shirt that belonged to Caroline's cousin Oliver and gave them to Seth. "Get into dry clothes, all three of you," she ordered. "I'll make hot willow-bark tea. It's the best thing to ward off a fever."

Caroline was glad to peel off her wet dress and to pull on thick, warm stockings. Soon everyone was gathered in the Abbotts' kitchen except Amelia Hathaway, who was napping upstairs. A big fire blazed in the hearth, and steam rose from mugs of tea. Caroline sat at the table with her winter cape draped over her shoulders. She let Seth and Rhonda repeat the tale of their adventure.

"Mercy!" Mrs. Hathaway said, shaking her head. "I will say a prayer of thanks tonight that none of you was hurt." She pressed her lips into a tight line as if imagining what might have been.

"It's sad to lose the skiff," Mama declared, "but look what was saved! That was sharp thinking."

Normally Caroline would glow with such praise from Mama, but she could still hear the harsh sound of splintering wood as the ax fell. She could still see the word *Sparrow* at a crazy angle above the water, shining in the sun.

Grandmother pulled a pan of gingerbread from the brick oven. She cut pieces and passed around plates. The spicy-sweet smell of warm gingerbread usually made Caroline's mouth water, but now she didn't have an appetite.

"The woodbox is almost empty," Grandmother murmured. "I'll just fetch a few more logs."

Caroline jumped to her feet. "I'll help," she said. She wanted a few moments alone with Grandmother, who often helped her sort through tangled feelings. She followed the old woman outside. Grandmother walked slowly, leaning on her cane. She was a small woman, with hands gnarled like tree roots and bones that often ached.

"Grandmother," Caroline began. "When I saw Papa's skiff ruined, left behind in the creek, I . . ." She stopped. It was hard to describe how she felt.

Grandmother took Caroline's chin in one hand and looked her straight in the eyes. "I know it's hard to lose the skiff, but you did *well* today," she said fiercely. "The British stole *White Gull*. That was one of the loveliest sloops your father ever built, and it's no doubt been renamed and put into the British fleet! Our enemy has stolen other ships as well. But today, thanks to you and your friends, they did not capture Irish Jack's bateau."

*I **am** proud of what we did*, Caroline thought. But the ache beneath her ribs didn't go away.

Caroline gathered an armload of wood, and Grandmother filled her own apron with smaller pieces. Before heading back inside, Caroline paused. "I'm tired," she said, scuffing a circle in the dirt with her toe. "After we take the wood in, I think I'll rest for a little while."

Upstairs, Caroline's cat, Inkpot, was curled into a ball on her bed. Caroline lay down and scratched him under the chin. "Oh, Inkpot," she whispered. "We saved Irish Jack's bateau and supplies, but we sank Papa's skiff! It's *ruined*."

Would Papa be disappointed in her when he heard what she'd done? Caroline wanted so much to talk with him. *If only he were here,* she thought. Tears spilled down her cheeks.

Then, for the first time, the fear that she had pushed away for so many months washed over her: *What if I never get the chance to talk to Papa again?* she thought. *What if he never comes home?*

Before Mama went back to the shipyard later that afternoon, she invited Seth to stay for supper. "Thank you, ma'am. I'd like that," he said. "And I'll be glad to help Caroline with chores until then."

Seth and Caroline grabbed empty buckets and headed outside. When they reached the well, Seth paused. "I'm sorry about the skiff, Caroline," he said. "I know it meant a lot to you."

Caroline nodded. "Papa made it." Her eyes blurred with tears. "Oh, Seth, what if Papa doesn't come back?"

Seth hooked a bucket handle onto a rope and

began lowering it into the well. "Your papa's coming back. Don't stop believing that, Caroline. And he'll understand that you had a hard choice to make when we saw that British sloop headed for the supply boat."

Caroline sighed. "Everything happened so fast."

"We had a grand victory this morning," Seth reminded her. "In fact, what happened back at Hickory Creek helped me make up my mind." He hauled up the full bucket, set it on the ground, and looked at Caroline. "I—I'm joining the navy."

Caroline's eyes widened. Seth? Joining the navy? She knew that boys even younger than Seth sometimes joined the navy. The smallest became "powder monkeys," scampering through a ship's cramped spaces to deliver ammunition during battles. Still, she'd never imagined Seth going off to fight. *But perhaps I should have,* she thought, remembering how he'd spoken of wanting to help drive the British back to Upper Canada.

"I've been thinking about it for some time," Seth said. "Seeing that British sloop chasing Irish Jack's bateau this morning—well, it made me angry! I am resolved to do whatever I can to help win this war."

Caroline wanted to say, *No, don't go! You might get hurt. And I'll miss you too much!* But she managed to swallow the words. "I'm proud of you, Seth," she said instead. "You'll do a fine job in the navy."

When Mama got home from the shipyard that evening, carrying a basket of salmon she'd purchased for supper, Caroline and Seth were hoeing weeds in the garden. "Wonderful!" Mama said. "Thank you, Seth."

Seth wiped his forehead, leaving a streak of dirt. "You've always treated me kindly, Mrs. Abbott. Since I've no family of my own, that means a lot."

"You're always welcome here," Mama assured him with a smile.

Caroline looked at Seth with a silent message: *Tell her your news.*

He nodded and told Mama about his decision to join the navy. "I've been walking my post route for four years," he explained. "Someone younger can take that job now."

"When are you leaving?" Mama asked.

"I'll send word to my employer, letting him know

he needs to find another post walker for my route," Seth said. "And I've a single day's worth of mail yet to deliver—the route closest to Sackets Harbor. Then I'll be free to enlist."

"I could deliver your mail tomorrow," Caroline offered. "I'd be proud to. That way you could enlist to fight the British one day sooner."

Mama hesitated.

"I won't get lost," Caroline said. "I know the route almost as well as Seth." She'd walked this part of his route with him several times, keeping him company.

"You'd have to get an early start," Seth told her. "It will be a long day of walking."

"I don't mind," Caroline insisted. "Please, Mama? I want to help."

Mama considered. "Very well," she said at last. "You're ten now. Old enough to take on that responsibility."

Caroline nodded. First thing in the morning, she'd be ready to go.

Into the Woods

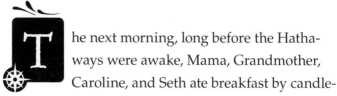

he next morning, long before the Hathaways were awake, Mama, Grandmother,
Caroline, and Seth ate breakfast by candle-
light. Then Seth went over the instructions for delivering mail. "Be sure to shout hello before you go into
the Randalls' clearing. Their dog doesn't like strangers
coming too close to the house. And—"

"I *know*," Caroline said. "You've told me these
things five times already!"

"I packed a lunch for you, Caroline," Grandmother
said. "Smoked fish, cheese, and bread. Seth, I packed
the same for you. I hear the food aboard navy ships
isn't so tasty."

"Thank you," Seth said. "It will likely be the best
meal I'll have for some time."

Mama was bustling around the kitchen. "Caroline?

Perhaps you should take a lantern."

"Must I?" Caroline asked. "It will be dawn soon, and I don't want to carry a lantern all day."

"Pack a candle, then," Mama said firmly. She held out a precious candle and several matches. Caroline tucked them into Seth's waxed canvas mailbag.

"Take a knife as well," Grandmother said. "While you're out, please cut some willow bark for me. Since it's so good for fighting fevers, I always want some handy."

Caroline nodded. "I'll gather what I can." She added a knife to the bag and slung the canvas strap over her shoulder.

The sun hadn't quite crept into the sky when the four of them walked outside, and Caroline shivered in the chilly gloom. Mama and Grandmother stopped to say good-bye at the front gate. "You come back when you can," Grandmother told Seth.

Seth smiled. "Yes, ma'am."

Mama grasped Caroline's shoulders. "Come straight home when you've finished your deliveries," she said sternly. "You've a long walk ahead of you, and you *must* be home before dark."

Caroline nodded. "I will."

"And stay well clear of strangers," Mama added. "These days there are spies about. Smugglers, too, trying to sneak weapons or supplies between New York and Upper Canada. And deserters—soldiers who have run away from their duty. Let them keep their bad business to themselves."

"I *will*," Caroline promised. "I'll be fine, Mama."

Caroline and Seth walked to Main Street together. From here, Seth would head down to the harbor. Caroline tried to give him a smile. "Please take good care of yourself," she said.

He held out a hand. Instead of taking it, Caroline threw her arms around her friend. Despite Grandmother's best efforts to feed Seth well, Caroline could feel every rib through his shirt. He gave her a quick, tight squeeze. Then he walked away.

Caroline took one deep breath before turning in the other direction. She had a job to do. Besides, staying busy and delivering the mail would help keep her from worrying too much about Seth.

Soon she left Sackets Harbor behind. *I'll try to deliver all of the mail before I eat lunch*, she decided. Then she'd turn around and head home.

As the sun rose, Caroline walked east on a narrow road so rutted and muddy that she was relieved to turn onto a hunting trail. In the thick forest, though, very little sunshine sifted through the leaves. Caroline pulled her wool shawl over her head to keep her ears warm.

Her first stop was a farm tucked into a small clearing, far from the nearest neighbor. A woman was planting her garden, and her husband and son were burning brush to make way for a new field. Caroline tried to walk around the blowing smoke as she approached the cabin. "I brought you a letter!" she called. The woman ran to greet her, smiling with pleasure. Caroline smiled back, feeling as if she'd done something good.

Caroline stopped at several more farms as she headed farther away from Sackets Harbor. After delivering her last piece of mail, she sat on a cliff overlooking Lake Ontario to eat lunch.

She recognized where she was, for she'd often seen this particular bit of high ground from the lake. *I'm not too far from Mallard Bay*, she realized. She remembered spring fishing trips with Papa on days like this, when the woods were full of blooming trees and birds sang pretty songs.

Caroline nibbled some cheese, thinking about the fish camp. She and Papa had usually been alone together at Mallard Bay. After losing the skiff, Caroline wanted more than ever to feel close to Papa. How she longed to visit the camp!

A tempting idea slipped into her mind. She was so close . . . why not just go?

A bold chipmunk skittered close, looking for stray crumbs. "But Mallard Bay is in the wrong direction," she told herself. Mama expected her to come straight home. And hadn't she promised Papa, when he was taken prisoner, that she'd obey Mama and Grandmother?

But Caroline didn't *want* to go straight home. More than anything, she wanted to go to Papa's fish camp. If she hurried, Mama would never know.

Caroline stuffed the rest of her lunch back into the sack, dusted her hands on her skirt, and got to her feet. She'd have to be quick. After hitching the bag over her shoulder, she started walking. She headed farther east instead of back toward Sackets Harbor. Caroline felt a little guilty about disobeying Mama, but the thought of visiting the fish camp again made her tingle with excitement.

Yet Mallard Bay seemed to be farther than she'd thought. She and Papa had always traveled there by boat, so she hadn't realized how long it would take to walk. The path wound through woods near the lake's edge, and with every twist and turn, she hoped to see the familiar fish camp appear in front of her. Each time, her hopes were disappointed.

Finally she thought, *Maybe I should turn back.* The sun was no longer directly overhead—the afternoon was passing. If she didn't get back home before dark, Mama would be angry! Besides, there were wild animals in the woods—cougars and wolves and bears. Caroline shivered. She didn't want to stumble into one of those in the dark! But she didn't want to turn back, either—not when she'd already come so far. *Surely* she was almost there.

She was getting thirsty, so when she spotted a narrow path leading from the main trail to the lake, she took it. The shoreline here was marshy, but the water was clear and cold. Caroline crouched at water's edge and cupped her hands. For a moment she let her hands stay underwater. How she loved Lake Ontario, and how she had loved sailing with Papa!

Suddenly she heard a low mutter of voices. She froze, eyes wide. Some of the cattails and tall reeds thrashed with a rustling sound.

"I'm bailing as fast as I can," a man's voice complained. "I can't keep up. We need to make camp for the night."

"It's not safe for us to make camp until dark," a second man hissed. "And keep your voice down!"

The front tip of a canoe appeared among the plants. For one startled moment, Caroline stared into the face of a stranger, who sat in the bow with his paddle. He looked as surprised as she felt. Then his face clouded with anger.

"You there!" he shouted. As the canoe slid from the cattails, the man in the back of the canoe came into view also. He scowled at her.

Caroline scrambled to her feet and raced into the woods. She didn't wait to hear if the men gave chase. Instead she plunged deeper into the underbrush. Brambles caught at her hands and cheeks. A low vine

or root caught her foot. She tripped and fell with a
noisy crash.

Ow! she whimpered silently. For a few moments she
couldn't move. Had the men heard her fall? She held
her breath, listening hard. She didn't hear anything.

Caroline blinked back tears of pain as she sat up.
Thorns had scratched her palms. Worse, her left arm
had hit a rock when she fell. Her dress was torn, and
blood oozed from a bad scrape near her elbow.

Oh no! she thought miserably. The rip in her sleeve
would not be easy to mend, and she saw that several
drops of blood stained the fabric. Mama and Grandmother would not be happy.

Caroline stumbled to her feet. Peering back through
the trees, she was relieved to see no sign of the two
men. They must have stayed down in the marsh. She
had to be nearly to Mallard Bay by now. Papa's fish
camp would be a good, safe place to clean the scrape
on her elbow. Then she would have to hurry home!

She glanced nervously at the sun again. If she
ran most of the way, walking only when she needed
to catch her breath, she should be able to get home
before dark.

But . . . where *was* the trail? Caroline looked around. *I'm lost!* she thought. Fear made her skin prickle and her breath come in little gasps.

She forced herself to take a deep breath and think calmly. *The trail follows the shoreline, roughly,* she reminded herself. Yet she was sure that she hadn't crossed the trail when she ran away from the strangers in the canoe. Looking over her shoulder through the trees, she saw the open sky over the lake. Carefully, she walked away from the lake in as straight a line as she could, making her way around trees and shrubs.

Just when she was starting to get frightened again, she climbed over a large rock and spotted the trail. Caroline blew out a long sigh of relief. She'd never been so glad to see that ribbon of tramped earth before!

Once back on the trail, Caroline was on her way. *Hurry-hurry-hurry*, a voice in her mind whispered. Finally she rounded a bend and saw the quiet, marshy waters of Mallard Bay ahead.

She'd reached Papa's fish camp!

At the Fish Camp

C aroline stopped on the path, taking in the familiar view. There was the little fire pit where Papa had fried his trout. The brush lean-to he'd constructed needed some repair, but it still stood nearby. The hollow log where he left fish lines and hooks seemed undisturbed.

Being here brought tears to her eyes. *This is a special place*, Caroline thought. She and Papa had shared many happy hours here. As she walked through the clearing and down the path to the lakeshore, she felt Papa's presence in her heart.

She knelt by the edge of the water and carefully washed the scrape on her arm. Although it still hurt, it had stopped bleeding. When she got home, Grandmother would apply a paste made of healing herbs. *And I need to get home fast*, Caroline told herself.

Golden sunlight slanted through the trees, casting long shadows.

Several scrubby willow trees grew near the water. Remembering Grandmother's request, Caroline quickly used the knife she'd brought to peel away bits of bark. Then she put them into her sack.

When she walked back to the clearing, Caroline paused for one moment more. She could almost hear Papa laughing. She could almost smell the wonderful aroma of fresh-roasted fish. "I'm still waiting for you to come home, Papa," she whispered. "I haven't given up hope."

As she reluctantly turned to leave, a low moaning sound made her freeze. Was an animal hurt nearby? She looked around the clearing but saw nothing.

The sound came once more. It seemed to be coming from the lean-to. Caroline's skin felt prickly again. She bent over slowly and peered into the lean-to. Someone was lying inside, half-covered with dead leaves.

Caroline didn't know what to do. The man had done his best to hide himself, which meant he didn't want anyone to see him. Was he a smuggler or a spy, or someone else up to no good?

She was about to run from the clearing when the man moaned again. Caroline felt troubled. He must be badly hurt, or sick. She tiptoed closer to the lean-to and peeked beneath the low roof.

A skinny man lay on a torn blanket. His eyes were closed, but he moved restlessly. Caroline studied him. His hair was long and uncombed. A beard covered his chin. The clothing she could see among the leaves was dirty and ragged, and his feet were bare. A tin cup rested on its side near his hand.

The man muttered something in his sleep. His forehead looked wet with sweat. Caroline wondered if he had a fever. She knelt beside the lean-to. The very least she could do for him was refill his cup before she left. *I'll stop at the nearest farm and tell the family about this man,* Caroline decided. The adults there would know what to do.

Holding her breath, she reached inside and retrieved the cup. Then she paused, squinting in the gloom. She didn't recognize the man. Still, there was something about him . . .

The man moaned again. "We must set sail," he muttered.

And then Caroline *knew*. Her heart banged against her ribs. "Papa? *Papa!*"

He didn't answer. She crawled to him and put one hand against his forehead as she'd seen Grandmother do. It *was* Papa—and he was burning with fever.

Caroline knew that if she didn't break the fever, Papa might die. She scrambled from the lean-to and raced to the lake. She ripped off a piece of her torn sleeve and wet it. Then she ran back to the lean-to and laid it over Papa's forehead.

What next? If only Grandmother were here! She would know what to do. Trembling with fear, Caroline tried to think calmly and remember what Grandmother had taught her.

Caroline quickly gathered firewood and then used one of the matches Mama had given her to start a fire. She fetched water from the lake and heated it in the tin cup. She crushed some of the willow bark she'd just gathered and added it to the water. Grandmother usually dried the bark before using it, but this would have to do.

When the tea was ready, Caroline crawled back into the lean-to. "You must drink this, Papa," she said gently. She cushioned his head on her lap and oh-so-slowly helped him sip the tea. Sometimes it spilled down Papa's cheek. By the time the cup was empty, though, she was sure that he'd swallowed some of the healing brew.

Caroline heated more water. Thank goodness she hadn't eaten all of her lunch! She crumbled the leftover bread and fish into the cup. Papa was skinny as an oar. Some soup would help. Her own stomach was beginning to growl, but she fed all of the food to Papa, one tiny sip at a time.

When the cup was empty, Papa seemed to settle into a deeper sleep. Caroline watched him breathe, her heart overflowing. Finding Papa felt like a miracle! But she knew he was very sick. *Did I find him just to lose him again?* Caroline wondered.

A while later, Papa moved. Caroline thought he opened his eyes for a moment, although it was hard to tell in the gloom. "Papa?" she whispered. "It's me, Caroline. Are you feeling better?" But he didn't answer.

By that time, full night was falling like a black blanket. Caroline lit the candle, dripped some hot wax on a flat stone, and used that to hold the candle upright.

She set the stone just inside the lean-to. The tiny light gave her a bit of comfort.

Although the night was cool, Papa was sweating. Was his fever breaking? She patted Papa's forehead dry with the hem of her skirt, but he didn't waken.

She lay down beside him. The night forest was full of rustles and strange noises, and her thoughts tumbled like pebbles in a creek. Mama and Grandmother must be dreadfully worried by now. *I'm sorry to frighten you,* Caroline told them silently, *but I must take care of Papa.*

Caroline opened her eyes to find a milky new dawn lighting the clearing. She sat up quickly and checked Papa. He was no longer restless, and his skin felt cooler beneath her fingers. Relief flooded through her. His fever had broken!

"Caroline?" Papa whispered. "Is that really you?"

Caroline didn't know whether to laugh or to cry. "It's me, Papa."

"Oh, my dear daughter, I feared I'd never see you again!" Papa blinked, as if he didn't believe his eyes. "How on earth did you find me?"

"I was delivering mail for Seth," Caroline explained. "I was supposed to go straight home yesterday, but I was so close to Mallard Bay, I decided to visit. I never imagined I'd find *you!*" A lump rose in her throat. "But—what are you doing here?"

"I escaped from the British, and I've been making my way home," Papa said in a husky voice. "I got this far, but I couldn't go any farther. I was very hungry. I hoped I might find my fishing line and hooks still tucked into the hollow log. But by the time I got here, I was too weak to use them."

"You've been ill," she told him. "You had a terrible fever last night. How long have you been traveling?"

"A long time," he murmured. "I've been moving slowly. You see, I broke my leg—"

Caroline caught her breath. "You broke your leg?"

"Months ago, now." Papa lifted his hand, then let it drop again. "But it didn't heal well."

Caroline grabbed his hand, almost afraid he'd disappear.

"Your mother, is she well?" Papa asked anxiously.

"She's fine," Caroline assured him. "Everyone is fine." At least they would be, once Caroline and Papa got home! "What *happened*, Papa? How did you escape?"

"The British in Kingston sent many of their prisoners east to Halifax last fall," Papa said. "I knew the trip would be my best chance to escape. We'd sailed far down the Saint Lawrence River before I got a good chance to try. One night I noticed that a guard had gotten drunk. I managed to yank the gun from his hands and crack him on the head with it."

Caroline's eyes went wide. It was hard to imagine her peaceful papa doing that! "Did you kill him?"

Papa shook his head. "No, dear child, but I imagine he lost his senses for a time. I dove over the side of the boat, swam to shore, and hid in the woods. Even though the moon was full that night, the guards didn't try to follow me. I suppose they decided that an American with no weapons or money or even a warm jacket, in British territory, with winter coming down hard, wasn't much of a threat."

Caroline shivered. "How ever did you survive? Where did you go? How—"

"I'll tell you everything in time, I promise." Papa squeezed Caroline's hand gently and closed his eyes. "I need to rest now."

Caroline waited until Papa was sleeping peacefully before creeping from the lean-to. Her head and her heart were full of worries. Mama and Grandmother must be terribly frightened by her absence, yet with Papa so weak and sick, how could she get him home?

If only I had a skiff or even a rowboat, she thought. Traveling by boat was far easier than trudging overland.

Caroline glanced back toward the lean-to, wondering what to do. She could leave Papa sleeping and run to get help, but what if a smuggler or other trouble-maker stumbled across the fish camp? What if Papa's fever grew worse again after she left?

I must stay here with Papa, she decided. *I must help him get stronger so that we can go home.*

While Papa slept, Caroline searched the woods nearby until she found a sturdy Y-shaped stick that she thought might work as a crutch. She stuffed Seth's mail sack with leaves and tied it into the notch to cushion Papa's arm when he leaned against it.

Papa's fishing gear was still in the hollow log. Caroline turned over stones until she found a worm to put on the hook. Then she went down to the shore to try her luck. It seemed to take a very long time to attract a fish, and several times she went back to the lean-to to make sure that Papa was sleeping. Finally she felt a tug on the line. A small whitefish was on the hook. She wanted to shout with joy, but it took all of her concentration to pull the line to shore without the fish getting away.

She had helped Papa and Grandmother clean fish many times. While the whitefish roasted on a stick beside the fire, she gathered some tender fiddlehead ferns growing near the campsite. When the fish was cooked, she made a cup of watery whitefish-and-fern soup for Papa.

By the time that was done, Papa was awake again. She found him sitting up inside the lean-to. "Oh, Papa," she said thankfully, "you're looking better."

"I'm feeling better too," Papa said. He accepted the soup she offered and slowly drank some. "My, that tastes good. I haven't had a warm meal in so long."

How had he ever survived? It hurt Caroline to imagine Papa hungry—and injured, too. "How did you break your leg?" she asked anxiously.

"I was so eager to cross the Saint Lawrence River and

reach American soil that I was careless," Papa told her.

"Careless?" Caroline asked. She'd never known Papa to be careless!

"After I escaped, I began making my way west, staying hidden, waiting for the river to freeze," Papa explained. "I set out as soon as the ice looked passable. I should have waited a few more days, though. I was almost to shore when the ice cracked and opened up right in front of me. I made a mighty leap, trying desperately to make it to the beach. I knew I'd freeze to death if I fell into that water."

Caroline's heart raced, as if she were facing the dangerous jump. Suppose he hadn't made it across?

Papa drained the last of the soup before continuing. "I did make the beach, but I landed on a rock and broke my leg. I would have died there if some Oneida men hadn't found me the next morning. One of them set my leg, and they took me to their village. I spent the winter there with the Indians. By the time the snow finally melted a few weeks ago, I knew my leg was as strong as it was going to get. So I thanked my Oneida friends and began walking home."

"Why didn't you send us word?" Caroline exclaimed.

"I didn't know whom I could trust," Papa said simply. "I knew that some of my old friends remained loyal to the British and might turn me in instead of helping me." He smiled at her. "I learned that lesson from the embroidered map you showed me when you visited me at the prison in Kingston."

Caroline felt proud to know that her handiwork had helped him. She had marked dangerous spots on the map she was embroidering of the eastern end of Lake Ontario. And she'd managed to show Papa the map—right under the guard's nose!

Papa squinted up at the sky. "Perhaps we should head for home."

"Are you feeling strong enough for that?" asked Caroline. It was hard enough to tend him here at the fish camp. She didn't want him to collapse when they were halfway home. "Perhaps we should wait until tomorrow."

Papa considered. "Let's start off and see how I do," he said finally. "Your poor mother must be beside herself with worry about you."

He crawled from the shelter, and she helped him get to his feet. He rested an arm across Caroline's shoulders and took one careful step, and then another. "I think I can do it," he said. "Your good care has made a world of difference."

Caroline fetched the crutch she'd made. "Try leaning on this," she said.

The crutch was too long for Papa to use comfortably. Caroline carefully placed it on a rock so that several inches stuck out over the end. *Careful!* she told herself. If she broke off too much, she'd have to search for another stick. That might take a long time.

Caroline held her breath. Then she snapped off the end of the crutch by stamping on it with one foot.

Papa gave it another try. "Perfect!" he said. "Nicely done, Caroline."

Caroline didn't like the way Papa limped, even with the crutch. She didn't like the way he pinched his mouth tight every time he put weight on his right leg.

"If there's any of that fish left, we should eat it now," Papa said. "And then we'll get started."

Caroline hesitated, then nodded. "All right, Papa," she said. "Let's get ready to go."

Twilight and rain fell together that evening as Caroline and Papa inched their way home. Despite the crutch, Papa limped more and more slowly. At one of the farms they passed, a woman gave them each a bowl of stew, but Papa refused her offer to spend the night. "We must get home," he insisted.

As they plodded forward, Papa's chin sagged toward his chest as if he was falling asleep. Caroline tried to keep him awake by telling stories about every thing that had happened at home since he'd been captured. She'd gotten to the fishing trip at Hickory Creek by the time they turned from the trail onto the main road to Sackets Harbor. Suddenly Caroline heard a *cra-ack*. Papa stumbled, then went down on one knee. The crutch had broken.

We must rest, Caroline thought. She looked around and pointed to a fallen log near the road. Thick tree branches overhead provided some shelter from the rain. "Let's sit for a moment, Papa."

When they were settled on the log, Papa gave her a weak smile. "So you and Seth and Rhonda had a good fishing trip?" he asked, encouraging her to continue the story.

"Well, no," Caroline confessed. She quickly told him about the British sloop that had tried to capture Irish Jack's bateau. "I knew we needed to block the channel," she said. "But—" Suddenly her voice caught. Part of her was eager to blurt out the truth about destroying the skiff. Part of her didn't want Papa to know.

"What's troubling you, daughter?" Papa asked softly.

"Oh, Papa!" Caroline cried. "To block the channel, we had to sink *Sparrow*! The sloop sailed away and the American supplies were saved, but we lost your skiff. I'm sorry. I had to make a choice very quickly, and . . ." Her voice trailed away.

Papa was quiet for several moments. *He is disappointed in me,* Caroline thought miserably.

Finally Papa said, "I think I know how you feel. When I was a prisoner on that British boat and saw a chance to escape, I had to act very quickly. Diving overboard *might* have been a bad decision. I might have died while I tried to get home. Sometimes, all we can do is take a chance and hope for the best."

Papa did understand! Relief rushed through Caroline. "Well, you are almost home now," she said stoutly. "Let's start walking again."

As they went on their way, Papa leaned more heavily on Caroline. Her knees trembled with the effort of keeping them both moving. It was getting dark, and the rain was falling harder. Soon they would both be soaked. In Papa's weakened state, that might bring back his fever.

Papa was determined, though. *And I'll keep going too,* Caroline promised herself fiercely. "Watch for the ruts, Papa. They're wicked."

It seemed to take forever, but finally Papa and Caroline reached Sackets Harbor. As they turned onto their lane, she heard someone calling her name. It was Mama! Caroline felt a new burst of energy. "Wait here," she told Papa. "Lean against this tree. I'll get help!"

Papa nodded. Caroline left him and stumbled toward their house. "Here!" she cried.

Mama appeared from the gloom. She carried a lantern, its tiny light flickering like a firefly. She set it down and grabbed Caroline into a crushing hug. "Oh, thank God, thank God," she whispered. "I thought I'd lost you."

Then Mama stepped back. Beneath the edge of her cap, her face was white. "Caroline Abbott, where have you been?" she demanded. "You frightened me out of my wits!"

"I'm so sorry, Mama," Caroline said quickly, "but *please* come with me. We need help!"

"We?" Mama asked, but Caroline was already splashing back through the mud toward Papa. She heard Mama close behind her.

In the dim light, they were almost upon Papa before she heard Mama gasp. "John?" she cried.

Papa opened his arms. "My sweet wife!"

Caroline felt a lump rise in her throat as she watched her parents cling to each other in the rain. "Thank you, God," she whispered. "Thank you for bringing Papa back to us."

Finally Mama pulled free. She wiped tears and raindrops from her cheeks. "Oh, John, I can scarcely believe it's you!" she said. "But how . . . where . . ."

"I'll tell you the whole story once we're home," Papa promised. "I can say that I wouldn't be here now if Caroline hadn't found me. I was sick and starving and too weak to travel any farther." He put one hand on Caroline's shoulder. "You saved my life, child."

Caroline pressed her cheek against Papa's hand. His words warmed her inside.

Mama looked at Caroline. "How did you ever . . . no, never mind now. I'll hear that story later, too. Now, let's get back to the house." She pulled one of Papa's arms over her shoulders so that she could help support him.

Caroline blinked back tears. It was still hard to believe that Papa was really, truly here!

She knew that the war was far from over. Rhonda's father was away fighting. Caroline's cousin Oliver had joined the navy, and Seth too. The British might attack Sackets Harbor at any moment.

But those troubles and worries can wait for tomorrow, Caroline thought as she slid her arm around her father's waist. "Lean on me too, Papa," she told him.

Together at last, the Abbott family headed toward home.

Signal Guns!

CHAPTER 6

T he next morning, Caroline tiptoed out of her house and closed the door behind her as silently as she could. It was hard to be quiet when she wanted to shout her good news from the rooftop! She hurried to the front gate and looked up and down the lane, hoping to see someone she knew passing by. Since America had gone to war with Great Britain, soldiers and sailors had flooded into the little village of Sackets Harbor, New York, and the lane was often bustling. Now, though, not a soul was in sight.

It's a fine May day, Caroline thought, *and I have no one to celebrate with!* Just when she was afraid she might burst, she spotted her neighbor coming outside with a market basket over her arm. Caroline slipped out the gate and raced after the plump woman. "Mrs. Shaw!" she called. *"Mrs. Shaw!"*

Mrs. Shaw turned and waited for Caroline to join her. "Gracious, Caroline," Mrs. Shaw said sternly. "It isn't seemly for young ladies to race about—"

"Papa is home!" Caroline cried. She was ready to take her neighbor's arm and dance a jig!

Mrs. Shaw stared at her with wide eyes. "Heaven be praised," she whispered. "Did the British release him after all this time?"

"No, he escaped!" Caroline bounced on her toes. "He got away last autumn, but he broke his leg in the wilderness and couldn't travel all winter. He's been making his way here ever since spring came. I found him at his old fish camp! And I helped him walk home last night."

Mrs. Shaw gave Caroline a quick hug. "Is he well?"

"He hasn't had enough to eat," Caroline told her. "And he needs to rest. He's sleeping now." Grandmother had sent Caroline outside to make sure that Papa could *continue* sleeping, actually, but Caroline didn't think Mrs. Shaw needed to know that.

Mrs. Shaw pulled out a handkerchief and wiped tears from her eyes. "I had given up hope," she admitted.

"*I* never did," Caroline said stoutly. It had been terribly hard to wait and wonder for so many months, but she had never lost hope.

"Well," Mrs. Shaw said, "you tell your father that I will bake a pie to welcome him home."

Caroline grinned. "I'll tell him," she promised.

Once Mrs. Shaw was on her way, Caroline tried to use up some of her bubbling energy by hoeing weeds in the garden. She and Grandmother had planted seeds earlier in the spring, and now tidy rows of tiny green seedlings marched across the soil. *Papa will eat some of those carrots and those peas!* Caroline thought happily. It felt like a miracle to have him home.

Hours seemed to pass before the kitchen door opened and Mama stepped outside. Caroline dropped the hoe and darted over to join her. "Is Papa awake?" she asked.

Mama smiled. "He is. After a good meal and a hot bath last night, he slept soundly. He's already looking much better. He's coming downstairs for breakfast."

Caroline bounced on her toes again. "May I sit with him?"

"Garden chores can wait," Mama agreed. She smiled and kissed the top of Caroline's head. "Let's go inside."

Caroline, Mama, Grandmother, and Papa lingered at the kitchen table as he ate breakfast. Caroline was grateful that Mrs. Hathaway and her daughters had kindly gone out to visit friends. "Your family needs a bit of privacy," Mrs. Hathaway had said.

Caroline sat on the bench next to Papa. *He's home,* she thought over and over. *Papa is home!*

"It does me more good than I can say to find my family well," Papa said. He finished a second biscuit. "But—I've been afraid to ask—what has happened to the shipyard?"

"Abbott's Shipyard is doing a brisk business," Mama told him.

"It is?" Papa blinked, as if that was far better news than he'd expected. "I feared that once the war began, no one would order any new ships. I imagined I would find the shipyard closed and silent, and all the workers gone."

Grandmother chuckled. "You have a pleasant surprise waiting!"

"You'll be proud of the men when you see everything they've done," Caroline promised him.

Papa smiled at her and stroked her hair. "No doubt you're right, Caroline," he said. "I am eager to inspect the yard." He folded his napkin and put it aside. "We'll go at once."

Mama looked concerned. "Perhaps that should wait. Don't you want a few more days of rest?"

"No indeed," Papa said. "I've spent almost a year wondering how my business has been faring. And I already feel like a new man."

"I'll come too!" Caroline exclaimed.

Once Caroline and Mama had fetched their shawls, the family set out, with Caroline on one arm and Mama on the other. *Papa does look like a new man*, Caroline thought, remembering how ragged he had looked when she'd found him at the fish camp. He still limped, and she realized sadly that he probably always would. But he had shaved, and Mama had cut his hair. His clothes looked big on his thin frame, but they were clean and free of holes.

"I hardly recognize our little village," Papa said, taking in the merchants' tents and hastily built taverns that had sprouted to serve all the soldiers, sailors, and shipbuilders who had arrived during his absence. Then the harbor came into view. Papa stopped walking and stared in astonishment.

Caroline tried to see the scene through Papa's eyes. Many things had changed while he was away. Each end of the harbor was now protected by a small log fort, with American flags proudly flying. She pointed to a narrow spit of land that stretched into the harbor. "We call that Navy Point now. See all those wooden buildings? Those are for military men and their supplies."

"So many soldiers and sailors are here now!" Papa marveled.

"Hundreds and hundreds," Caroline told him. "But a lot of them—like Lieutenant Hathaway—are away right now. They sailed off to Upper Canada more than a month ago to capture some forts." She tried to hide a shiver. She didn't like having so many sailors and soldiers gone. What if the British attacked?

Papa didn't seem to notice her unease. "And it

seems that Abbott's is no longer the only shipyard in Sackets Harbor," he said. He stared at a new shipyard next to his own. It was much bigger than Abbott's and bustling with activity.

"The navy has established its own yard," Mama told him. "There are hundreds of shipwrights and carpenters in the village now."

Papa stared with admiration at a huge ship under construction in the navy yard. Caroline told him, "That frigate will be the mightiest ship ever to sail the Great Lakes! It's going to have twenty-eight cannons."

"Well, that should give the British trouble!" Papa said, rubbing his jaw.

"*Our* shipyard is giving the British trouble, too," Caroline told him proudly. "We're not making mer- chant sloops and schooners anymore. We're building gunboats for the navy."

Papa shook his head, as if trying to take in all the changes. "This is a much better homecoming than I could have imagined," he said.

Caroline slipped her arm through his. "Let's go see the men," she said. "They'll have a lot to show you."

The workmen at Abbott's were overjoyed to see

Papa. Caroline laughed as they whooped and cheered and tossed their hats into the air. *How joyful it must be for Papa,* she thought, *to find his workers still here!*

Mr. Tate pumped Papa's hand. "I always knew you'd come home, sir," he declared. "Indeed I did." His eyes sparkled with unshed tears.

For a moment Papa seemed unable to find words. He clenched Mr. Tate's hand. Caroline could see that her father was overwhelmed with emotion.

Finally Papa cleared his throat. "I'm very glad to be here," he said in a husky voice. "Now, I'd like to inspect the yard."

Mr. Tate showed him the gunboat the men were building. He explained everything they had learned as they switched from making trading ships to constructing heavy military boats. Caroline saw the workers listening carefully, as if hoping that Papa would approve of everything that had been done in his absence.

When the tour was complete, Papa declared, "I am more proud of you all than I can say. I spent months fearing that Abbott's Shipyard was no more. Instead, you've been helping to defend our country from our enemy!"

The men grinned and elbowed each other. Caroline was proud of them, too. She *knew* how hard they'd worked. She'd watched them.

Then Papa went to the office, and Mama showed him how she'd kept the books. "You managed all this?" Papa asked.

"Mama took charge right away," Caroline told him. "She's handled the contracts and made sure the men had the supplies they needed."

Papa looked startled. "I see," he said.

"I had a lot of help," Mama explained. "Mr. Tate watched over the workers, and Caroline helped me watch over the business accounts."

"Caroline?" Papa sounded taken aback, and he looked at her with an expression she didn't recognize. "My little girl, helping with the accounts?"

"I just tried to be helpful," Caroline said quickly. "I made copies of letters that Mama needed to send and checked the sums in the ledgers." She knew that Mama had given her those tasks largely so that Caroline could practice her penmanship and arithmetic. Even so, she'd taken pride in the work. She watched Papa, anxious to know that he was proud of her and of Mama, too.

"I see that I have much to learn," Papa said quietly. He didn't look at Caroline but instead settled on the high stool in front of his desk. He opened a ledger and began looking through the records.

"Caroline, perhaps you and I should take a stroll down the dock," Mama said. "It's such a fine day."

Caroline followed Mama outside. "Is something wrong?" she asked as she and Mama walked away from the office. "Is Papa displeased?"

"Not at all," Mama assured her. "You and I must try to remember that for all these months, Papa feared that his business would fail without him. He didn't expect to find Abbott's Shipyard busier than ever."

Caroline was still confused. "But . . . that's *good* news. I thought he would be happy!"

"He will be," Mama said. "But we must give Papa time to learn about all the changes that have taken place while he was away. Can you be patient with him?"

"Of course," Caroline said firmly. She would do anything she could to help Papa.

❊

The next morning, Caroline came downstairs at dawn and found Grandmother and Mrs. Hathaway making breakfast. The bacon sizzling over the fire smelled so good that Caroline's stomach growled.

"Please set the dining-room table," Grandmother told Caroline. "Now that your father is home, we've too many people to fit here in the kitchen."

Once everyone had gathered around the table, Caroline introduced the boarders. "Papa, this is Mrs. Hathaway and Rhonda and Amelia." She beamed. For many months, the Hathaways had heard stories about Papa. Now they could meet him in person!

Little Amelia was very quiet, sucking her thumb and watching him closely. Rhonda seemed unusually shy as well. "A pleasure to meet you, sir," she said. After a quick nod, she looked down at her plate.

Caroline nudged Rhonda under the table with her knee. Usually that would make Rhonda giggle and nudge back even harder. Today, though, Rhonda didn't respond. Caroline was puzzled by her friend's mood.

Suddenly, Caroline realized why Rhonda was being quiet. *Everything's turned upside down*, Caroline thought. *I used to envy Rhonda because **her** father was nearby.* Now

Papa was home, and Rhonda's father was off on a dangerous expedition. Caroline leaned close enough to whisper in her friend's ear, "Your father will be back soon, and—"

Boom! Boom! Caroline looked up sharply and clapped her hands over her ears as cannon fire shuddered through the air. The windowpanes rattled, and it felt as if her bones rattled too.

Papa dropped his fork with a clatter. Mama's face went white.

Not today, Caroline thought. She felt numb with disbelief. "Those shots came from the big guns at the forts," she said. "Sackets Harbor must be under attack!"

Papa's hands curled into fists. His face settled into hard lines.

Caroline jumped to her feet. She ran from the dining room and out the front door. She had to find out what was happening! Her family and the Hathaways joined her just as a young man on horseback clattered toward them.

Papa stepped to the gate and waved a hand. "*Sir!*" he barked in his ship-captain voice. "What's happening?"

Signal Guns!

The young man pulled his horse to a stop.
"A British fleet has been sighted about seven miles
from here," he told them, breathing hard. "I'm with
the militia, on my way to spread the word."

"How large is the fleet?" Papa demanded.

"There are probably a thousand enemy men out
there," the militiaman said. "And when they land,
they'll have their ships' cannons to protect them."

A thousand men? Caroline felt anger boil up inside.
"Hateful British! I wish they would just leave us *alone!*"

Papa squinted the way he sometimes did when he
was sailing a ship and making a judgment about the
weather. "There's no wind," he said.

"Aye," the soldier agreed. "Those ships can't move
with no wind in their sails. That gives us some time
to call in the militia. Now, I must be off." He kicked
his horse to a gallop, and everyone watched him
pound away.

Mama murmured, "Thank heavens the British
weren't able to surprise our men."

"But the wind could start blowing again any
moment!" Caroline said.

"It could." Papa nodded. "The wind could pick up

again an hour from now, or a day from now. We must use whatever time we have to prepare for the attack."

Grandmother leaned on her cane with both hands. "We've known they would come sooner or later," she said. "They're after that big new frigate the navy's building, I'd wager."

"But most of our soldiers and sailors are away!" Rhonda cried. "There's hardly anyone left to defend us!"

"Those alarm guns were meant to call out the militia," Grandmother reminded Rhonda. "And riders like that young man will be on their way to distant farms where the men might not hear the guns. Our militiamen will be ready to meet the British."

Caroline understood why Rhonda sounded frightened. She was frightened, too. She had seen the militia drilling in town, practicing for a battle. The farmers and workmen were not nearly as well trained as the army and navy men.

Another deafening *boom-boom* sounded as the signal guns repeated their message. "Come, girls," Mrs. Hathaway said quietly to Rhonda and Amelia. She shepherded her daughters back inside.

Caroline glanced at Papa. He looked grim. *What a terrible homecoming,* Caroline thought.

For a long moment, no one spoke. Then Papa turned to his wife. "I must go."

"What?" Mama gasped.

"Go where?" Caroline asked at the same time.

Papa said, "To volunteer with the militia."

"Papa, no!" Caroline cried. How could he leave? She'd just gotten him back!

Mama clutched his arm. "You're not yet well."

"I'm well enough," Papa said. "I can handle a musket. Sackets Harbor needs every man to fight."

Caroline grabbed Papa's free hand. *If I never let go,* she thought, *maybe Papa won't leave.* She watched her parents anxiously.

"I don't *want* to go," Papa said to them. "But I think you understand why I must."

"But you just got home," Caroline protested. "It's not *fair*!"

"It isn't fair," Papa agreed. He squeezed her hand. "But life is not always fair, especially in times of war."

Mama still looked worried, but she nodded. "Very well," she said. "You join the militia and defend the village. But the gunboat and our shipbuilding supplies must be protected as well. I'll keep watch at the ship-yard."

Papa shook his head. "You will not! Mr. Tate and the men will defend the shipyard. You and your mother and Caroline must take shelter in the root cellar." He put one arm around Caroline's shoulders. She burrowed closer, wishing she could stay beside him forever.

Papa added, "I don't want to join the militia with-out knowing that all of you are safely away from the fighting."

He sounded so worried that Caroline knew she had to help ease his mind. "We'll stay safe," she promised, but it was hard to squeeze the words around the lump in her throat.

Bad News at the Shipyard

W hen the Abbotts went back inside, they found the Hathaways in the hallway with packed carpetbags. "My husband gave me firm instructions about what to do during an attack," Mrs. Hathaway explained. "I must take the girls inland, away from the fighting. We'll find shelter with a farm family we met as we traveled here last fall." She looked at Mama. "We could all go together."

"Thank you for the offer," Mama told her. "But we have property to protect. I will not leave Sackets Harbor."

Caroline knew that many women and children would be leaving the village, hoping to get far away before the fighting started. She was frightened too, but like Mama, she didn't want to leave her home.

"We'll be safe enough in the root cellar," Grandmother added briskly. "Once the Americans drive the British away, we'll be waiting for your return."

"Very well." Mrs. Hathaway nodded. "Be safe, my dear friends. God willing, we'll all be together again."

Rhonda and Caroline hugged each other. "Come back soon," Caroline whispered.

"As soon as we can," Rhonda whispered back. Mrs. Hathaway led her daughters away.

Caroline stayed close to Papa as he fetched his old musket, cleaned it well, and packed ammunition in a pouch. She could hardly believe that Papa was leaving again.

Once his preparations were made, Papa led his family outside. Scary pictures formed in Caroline's mind. What if Papa were wounded in battle? What if he got *killed*? She threw her arms around him. "I wish you weren't going!"

"There, now." Papa stroked her hair. "A man must protect his home and family. I need to do my part."

Caroline struggled to keep from crying. *Don't make this harder on Papa than it is already,* she told herself sternly, but she couldn't seem to loosen her grip around Papa's waist.

He gently pulled away from her. "You be careful, daughter," he said. "Help your mama and grandmother as best you can."

"I—I will," Caroline promised. She blinked hard as her eyes filled with tears.

"Once we've sent the British back to Upper Canada, I will lay down my musket and get back to work as a shipbuilder," he added. "Remembering busy days at Abbott's Shipyard helped me survive while I was a prisoner. Imagining us all working there together will help me survive this day, too."

Papa kissed Mama, Grandmother, and Caroline good-bye. Then he limped away. The lane was busy with traffic now—militiamen rushing to their posts, riders carrying news, women and children hurrying away from the village with bundles and sacks. As Caroline watched, Papa was quickly swallowed by the crowd.

Mama and Grandmother turned to go inside. Caroline paused, sniffing the air to see if a breeze had come up yet. The morning was heavy and still, with low clouds that threatened rain. Every leaf on every tree hung motionless.

The British must still be offshore, impatiently waiting for a wind to fill their sails, thought Caroline. *All **we** can do now is wait, too.* There was no way to predict when a wind might blow the British fleet toward Sackets Harbor.

When Caroline followed Mama and Grandmother back inside, the house seemed terribly silent. *What should I do now?* Caroline wondered, twisting her hands together. She wished there were something she could do to help Papa and the other American fighters. It was so hard to simply wait for the attack to begin!

Grandmother gave Caroline a meaningful look. "At such times, it's best to stay busy. I've already started heating the bake oven. I'll make a double batch of bread today. There may be hungry soldiers needing food before too long."

Mama had been standing very still, her head tipped thoughtfully to one side. Suddenly she reached for her bonnet and cape, which were hanging on a stand by the front door.

"Mama?" Caroline asked. "Where are you going?"

"I am going to the shipyard," Mama said.

Grandmother chuckled and nodded, as if she'd been expecting this.

Caroline, though, had not. "But Papa said—"

"Papa said the workers would guard the gunboat and building supplies," Mama said. "And they will. But I've been thinking. Papa hasn't seen all the important records that are stored in the office now. Designs for gunboats, instructions from the navy—the British would probably value those things even more than the gunboat itself."

Caroline pressed a hand over her mouth. She hadn't thought about that! But Mama was right—if the British got their hands on the plans created by America's finest shipbuilders, they could use the new ideas and designs in their *own* ships.

"I am determined to remove as many documents as I can before the wind picks up," Mama added. "We'll hide them here at home."

Caroline's spirits rose. Surely Papa would understand why Mama was acting against his instructions. Besides, she welcomed the idea of *doing* something to help beat the British. "May I come with you? *Please?* I want to help!"

"Yes indeed," Mama said. "Go fetch the big gathering baskets from the kitchen."

As Caroline raced to do Mama's bidding, she sent a silent message to the British men on their ships. *We will not give up easily*, she warned them. The Abbotts, each in their own way, were ready to fight.

In a few minutes Caroline and Mama set off, each carrying two empty baskets. A light rain drizzled from the clouds, but the air remained still. Caroline pressed close to Mama, for Main Street was mobbed. Men on horseback trotted past. Army men drove supply wagons through town, trying to remove anything the British might steal. Near the harbor, traffic had halted altogether because a family's cart had broken its axle.

"This way!" Mama called, leading Caroline through the noisy commotion. Caroline clutched her baskets tightly so that they wouldn't get jostled from her hands.

When they reached Abbott's, Caroline saw the workers standing guard around the shipyard, armed with broadaxes and mallets. It hurt Caroline's heart to see shipbuilding tools used as weapons, but she was more proud of the men than ever.

Mr. Tate hurried to greet them, carrying his ancient musket. "I didn't expect to see you, ma'am!" he exclaimed. "And Miss Caroline as well! Where is Mr. Abbott?"

"Papa left to join the militia," Caroline told him.

Mr. Tate shook his head. "And him just newly arrived home? *Blast* the British."

"I see that you and the men are set to defend the yard," Mama said. "Well done. Caroline and I are going to haul off whatever records and plans we can carry."

Mr. Tate gave a quick, satisfied nod. "I'll leave you to it," he said.

Caroline and Mama hurried into the office. "Roll up those plans," Mama said, pointing to the large sketches Mr. Tate had made to guide the carpenters building the gunboat outside. "I'll gather the ledgers."

Caroline did as she was told, quickly rolling up the large pieces of parchment and tying them with string. Then she filled her baskets with account books and the letters that Mama had exchanged with the U.S. Navy officers who had hired Abbott's to build gunboats.

With their loaded baskets, Caroline and Mama struggled more than ever to make their way through the crowded streets. By the time they reached home, Caroline's arms ached. Her toes ached, too, for several people had stepped on them as she'd wormed her way through the crowds.

Grandmother met them at the kitchen door. "Empty the baskets, and leave everything to me," she said. "I know a thing or two about hiding valuables from British soldiers."

Caroline didn't doubt that! Grandmother had lived through the American Revolution thirty years earlier, doing everything she could to help defeat the British. "We're going back for another load," Caroline told her. She piled the contents of her baskets on the kitchen table.

Grandmother gave Mama a sideways glance. There was a question in her eyes.

"There is still no wind," Mama told her. Caroline nodded. She and Mama were paying attention to the weather. If even a breath of wind came up, they'd notice right away.

"Get on with it, then." Grandmother made a shoo-ing gesture.

Caroline and Mama made their way back to the harbor. Suddenly Caroline heard a faint rattle of musket fire in the distance.

"I don't like the sound of that," Mama said grimly.

"How could there be fighting already?" Caroline burst out. "I thought the British were stuck offshore!" Were British soldiers already marching toward Sackets Harbor? Was Papa already in the midst of fighting, already in danger? Caroline shivered. They had no way of knowing what was happening even a few miles away.

"Perhaps the British got tired of waiting and rowed some men ashore," Mama said. "If so, they can't have landed many soldiers. Still, we must hurry." She grabbed Caroline's arm as they elbowed their way toward the yard. Caroline was glad to feel Mama's firm grasp.

When they reached Abbott's again, Caroline expected to see the workers still standing guard. Instead, the men had gathered in a clump near the entrance. Mr. Tate seemed to be arguing with a man in an American military uniform. *Oh no*, Caroline thought. *What now?*

Mama hurried to join the conversation. Caroline wanted to hear too, and followed on Mama's heels. Caroline could tell by the fancy braid on the soldier's coat that he was an officer. He had gray hair, and there were dark circles beneath his eyes.

"Gentlemen!" Mama said in a tone that stopped the discussion. She introduced herself to the officer. "I'm in charge of the shipyard when my husband is away," she told him. "What's happening?" She gestured toward the far-off sound of muskets.

"A few dozen British men and some of their Indian allies rowed ashore several miles west of here," the officer said. "As soon as the wind picks up, though, the British fleet will surely head for Sackets Harbor and try to land a huge force near the village."

Caroline swallowed hard as she imagined hundreds of British soldiers and sailors fighting their way into her village. The drizzle suddenly seemed very cold.

Mama pinched her lips together for a moment. Then she said, "I understand, sir. But what is your business here?"

The officer waved his hand toward the shipyard. "I need these men to help defend Navy Point."

Caroline caught her breath. She saw the men exchanging worried glances and heard them muttering in protest. "We're needed here, to guard the gunboat!" one of the carpenters shouted.

"With so many of the American troops away, our position is desperate," the officer snapped. "We need every man to fight."

"But—but sir," Caroline stammered, "who will defend our shipyard?"

"Let us pray the British won't reach the shipyards," he said. "Now, all of you men—line up. Bring whatever weapons you have."

Mr. Tate looked at Mama. "Ma'am?"

"Do as he says," Mama told him quietly. She turned to the workers. "Please take care of yourselves."

With dismay, Caroline watched the shipbuilders form a ragged line. These were the men who'd kept Abbott's Shipyard going, who had been kind and patient with her, who had lifted her spirits during the difficult last year. Now they were ready to do what was necessary to defend Sackets Harbor. She knew that the men would do Abbott's proud, just as they always had, but she hated to see them go.

Hosea Barton, the sailmaker, paused beside her. "Don't worry, Miss Caroline. We'll be back. We've got a gunboat to finish."

Mr. Tate was the last to leave. "Mrs. Abbott, I'm sorry," he said. "What will you do?"

"I'll do whatever I must," Mama said. Her voice was calm, but Caroline saw that she'd clenched folds of her cape into her fists. "Thank you, sir, for everything."

Mr. Tate nodded, tugged his hat down over his eyes, and propped his musket over one shoulder. Then he turned and joined the other men as they tramped away.

Caroline and Mama stood still and watched them go. The day's noise and commotion suddenly seemed distant. *I've never seen the shipyard empty before*, Caroline thought. She'd visited Abbott's in the morning, at midday, in the evening . . . and always, *always*, at least some of the men were there.

Now Abbott's was quiet. The yard was deserted. A battle was brewing, and Caroline and Mama were alone.

Terrible Orders

Caroline and Mama watched the workers until they disappeared from view. The musket fire in the distance had stopped. The new silence seemed terrible and threatening.

Finally Mama turned toward the office. "We must make haste," she said. "I want you to take one last batch of records home."

Caroline's mouth went dry as she realized that Mama was sending her back alone. She remembered what Mama had told Mr. Tate: *I'll do whatever I must.*

Mama put her hands on Caroline's shoulders and looked her straight in the eye. "I'm staying here at the yard."

"But, Mama," Caroline protested, "Papa told us to take shelter in the root cellar, where we'll be safe!"

"Yes, he did," Mama said soberly. "But Papa didn't

know that all the workers would be pulled away to help defend the village. The situation has changed, Caroline. Now I must do what I think is best. I trust that Papa will understand."

Caroline hated leaving Mama all alone at the shipyard. Still, she knew that Mama needed help, not arguments, so she held her protests inside. "Yes, Mama," she said reluctantly. "I'll go."

In the office, Caroline helped pack two baskets with the last ledger and letters. "Once you're back at the house," Mama said, "take Grandmother into the root cellar. A wind might spring up at any minute and fill those British sails!" After kissing Caroline on the forehead, Mama gave her a little push toward the door.

Caroline hurried back through Sackets Harbor. There were no women or children in sight. Caroline knew that they were either safely away or sheltering inside their own cellars by now. It felt strange, and a little spooky, to be alone among soldiers and militiamen who were thinking only of battle. When Caroline reached her house, she scurried inside and closed the door behind her with a *whoosh* of relief.

When she told Grandmother about Mama's decision,

the old woman did not look surprised. "I wouldn't expect your mother to do anything less," Grandmother said. "She's a brave woman."

Caroline nodded. Grandmother and Mama were *both* brave women. Caroline hoped that she might one day prove herself to be as smart and courageous as they were.

Grandmother rubbed her chin, looking about the kitchen. "There's no telling how long she'll have to stay at the shipyard," she murmured. "Tell me, Caroline, is there any wind yet?"

"No, ma'am," Caroline said. "The lake is as still as a bowl of milk."

"Good. I want to send some food and a blanket down to your mother. Will you make one more trip to the yard?" Grandmother looked at her intently.

Caroline blinked in surprise. Mama had instructed her to stay safely at home until the battle was over! *But Grandmother is right*, Caroline thought. There was no way to know how long Mama might be alone at the shipyard. And Mama had said that sometimes, in difficult situations, people need to make their own choices.

Caroline squared her shoulders. "Yes, I will," she told Grandmother. "I'll run like a deer."

Grandmother smiled. "That's the spirit," she said. "I've got beans and bacon warm over the fire. Fetch a plate and have a good meal yourself, and I'll prepare some supplies for your mother."

Caroline hadn't thought she was hungry, but with one bite of the sweet and salty baked beans, she changed her mind. By the time she'd gobbled her helping and eaten a piece of warm bread dripping with butter, Grandmother had joined her again.

"Here's the basket," Grandmother began. "I want you to see what I've packed."

Caroline scrambled to her feet, wiping her mouth with a napkin. "I'm sure Mama will be pleased with whatever you send, Grandmother."

"I want you to see what I've packed," Grandmother repeated. Her voice was unusually slow and forceful.

Caroline went still. Something was on Grandmother's mind.

"I've put in two loaves of bread, the last of the dried apples, and some smoked fish." Grandmother gestured at each of the items. Then she lifted the corner of a cloth she'd put under the food. "And something else your mama might need."

Caroline's eyes went wide as she saw the silver glint of metal. Grandmother had hidden a pistol under the cloth. Nestled beside it was a little sack that no doubt held ammunition.

Grandmother tucked the cloth back in place. "You must deliver this to your mother's hands."

"Yes, ma'am," Caroline whispered. The sight of the gun made her feel shivery inside. Many years ago, Papa had ordered Caroline not to touch either of his guns, and she never had. *But I must carry this pistol to Mama*, she thought. The only way Mama would have a gun to help defend Abbott's was if Caroline took it to her.

"One more thing." Grandmother cupped Caroline's face in her hands. "I'm an old woman. I've lived through more than one battle. As soon as trouble starts, I will settle myself in the root cellar, safe from enemy gunfire. I'm not afraid to be alone. Do you understand?"

Caroline swallowed hard. Grandmother's eyes held everything that she didn't say: *Make your own decision about coming home, my girl. If you feel that you should stay with your mama, do not worry about me.* Now Caroline understood why Grandmother had insisted that she eat a hearty meal before heading back to the shipyard.

It took Caroline a moment to find her voice. Finally she took a deep breath. "Yes, Grandmother," she said. "I understand."

"Good girl." Grandmother patted Caroline's cheek.

Caroline put on her cloak, picked up the blanket roll that Grandmother had prepared, and hooked the basket handle over one arm. "I'll do my best," she promised.

"I know you will." Grandmother nodded. "Off you go."

Caroline hurried back to Abbott's Shipyard. The office was on the ground floor of the main shipyard building, close to the street. When Caroline looked inside, she found the room empty. Next she checked the workshops behind the office. They were empty too. Perhaps Mama was up in the sail loft. The big room where Hosea stitched huge sails was on the second story of the building. From the window there, Mama would be able to see the half-built gunboat in the yard below. She'd also be able to see the harbor.

Mama came running when she heard footsteps on the stairs. "Caroline!" she cried. "I expected you to stay home!"

"I know," Caroline said quickly. "But Grandmother asked me to bring you some supplies." She put the basket on a bench and showed Mama what had been packed inside.

"That was thoughtful," Mama said as she saw the food. "And—ah." Caroline had lifted the cloth, revealing the pistol. Mama pulled the gun free, loaded it, and slipped it into a pocket.

Caroline looked around the empty loft. Through the window, she could see the empty yard. *I need to stay here*, Caroline thought. She hoped Mama wouldn't order her to go back home. She felt her hands tremble and clutched them together behind her back so that Mama wouldn't see.

Then Caroline lifted her chin. "Grandmother told me she would be fine alone," she said firmly. "You need help more than she does. I'm going to stay here with you, Mama."

For a moment Caroline thought Mama was going to disagree. Caroline forced herself to hold her mother's gaze. *I can do it,* she told Mama silently. *I can be brave and help protect Abbott's Shipyard.*

Finally Mama nodded. "Very well, Caroline," she said. "Thank you. The yard is a lonely place with all the men gone. I'll be glad of your company."

Mama stayed up in the sail loft, where she could see the street and yard below and look out on the harbor. Caroline kept watch from the office doorway, wrapped in her cloak. Militiamen jogged past all afternoon, splashing through puddles in ones and twos and groups. They'd come from distant farms and villages to join the line of men defending Sackets Harbor. The sight of the men, hard-faced and ready to fight, made Caroline's stomach tumble. Sometimes she glanced up for reassurance at the "Abbott's" sign that hung over the entrance to the yard. *Abbott's Shipyard is here to stay,* she thought stubbornly, *and so am I.*

Once, an army officer hurried by. "Any news?" Caroline called.

"Those British ships still can't move," he told her. "Their sails are hanging limp as laundry on the line."

Caroline *almost* wished the wind would pick up. It was so difficult to simply wait, wait, *wait*!

The sun was setting when a young man in navy uniform raced into Abbott's Shipyard, his hat pulled low against the light rain. "Halloo the yard!" he hollered. "Mrs. Abbott?" He leaned over, panting for breath.

Caroline quickly stepped from the doorway and introduced herself. "My mother is keeping watch upstairs," she told him.

Mama leaned out the window. "I'll be right down, Corporal Meyers!" she called. A few moments later, she hurried from the building and joined them. "What's the news?" she asked at once.

"You've probably heard that a small British force landed west of here this morning," Corporal Meyers said.

"What happened?" Caroline asked anxiously.

"The fighting went badly for us," he said. "Some of the Americans retreated. Others surrendered, blast their hides."

Caroline leaned against Mama.

"As soon as the weather changes, the British will

surely attack Sackets Harbor," Corporal Meyers continued. "We're preparing bonfires in the navy shipyard."

"Preparing *bonfires*?" Caroline asked. "Why?"

Corporal Meyers jerked his head toward the huge warship that was under construction in the navy yard. "If the British fight their way through the line of Americans defending the harbor, we will burn the navy shipyard and destroy our new frigate. Whatever else happens, we must not let that ship fall into enemy hands!"

Caroline followed his gaze. The navy workers had framed up the ship and begun nailing planks in place. She knew the Americans needed that mighty ship to take control of Lake Ontario and help win the war.

"Ma'am, you must make the same plans," Corporal Meyers told Mama. "Prepare bonfires, and torches as well."

Caroline stared at him. His words were quite clear, and yet she had a hard time taking in his meaning. *He wants us to burn Abbott's if our soldiers can't stop the British*, she thought. She felt numb.

"I understand," Mama told Corporal Meyers. She reached for Caroline's hand and squeezed. "We'll prepare."

Caroline opened her mouth, but no words came out. She felt as if the world were suddenly spinning in circles and the only thing keeping her feet planted on the ground was Mama's grip.

"If all is lost, we'll set fire to the barracks and storehouses on Navy Point," the corporal told them. "You'll see the flames. That will be your signal."

Mama nodded. "Very well."

"May God protect us," Corporal Meyers said. For just a moment, he looked more like a frightened farmboy than a military man. Then he tipped his hat before running off again.

"Mama?" Caroline's voice shook. "Did you really mean . . . ?" She couldn't finish the sentence.

"We must not let Abbott's fall into enemy hands!" Mama said fiercely. "The gunboat, all our tools and supplies—it's better to destroy them than let the British take them and use them against us."

Caroline desperately wanted to pretend that none of this was happening. How could her mother even consider this dreadful thing? "Oh, Mama," she said, "we *can't* burn the shipyard!"

"I pray we won't have to," Mama replied. "But we must be prepared to do so if necessary."

In the twilight, Caroline looked around the yard. Papa had worked for years to build his business. And Mama and the Abbott's men had worked night and day to keep it going while they waited for Papa to come home. *How can we destroy it?* she asked herself. How would Papa feel if he returned and saw nothing but ashes?

"Mama . . ." Caroline's throat felt thick with panic. "Papa's heart will break if we burn the yard!"

For a long moment, Mama stared silently at the shipyard. "I know," she said finally. "But if we must, I think Papa will understand that we did what we had to do."

Caroline still wasn't sure. "Mama? How do you know when it's right to do what you're told, and when to decide for yourself?"

Mama looked down and held Caroline's gaze. "It is sometimes very difficult," she admitted. "I try to use both my mind and my heart."

Caroline was silent. Her mind said that burning the shipyard if the Americans were defeated was the right thing to do. Her heart said that burning the shipyard would be horribly wrong.

"I wish Papa were here," Caroline whispered.

"I wish he were here, too," Mama said. "But he isn't, so we must simply do the best we can." She blew out a long breath before adding, "You chose to stay here with me, Caroline. Now you must stand tall, because I truly need your help."

For a moment Caroline wished she *had* stayed at home with Grandmother. If she had, she wouldn't have to face Corporal Meyers' terrible orders.

Seconds seemed to tick past in Caroline's mind, loud as a mantel clock. Finally she thought, *Mama is right.* She had chosen to stay. Now she had to be steady and face whatever had to be faced.

"I'll help you, Mama," Caroline said at last. Her voice still shook a little, and she struggled to firm it up. "Tell me what I need to do."

The Battle

A s twilight's shadows stretched across the shipyard, Caroline and Mama got busy gathering wood. "We'll start the bonfire," Mama said, "and keep it blazing so that we can light torches quickly if we need to burn the yard."

Caroline knew it wouldn't be hard to burn the shipyard to the ground. Almost everything—the workshops, the storage sheds, and the gunboat itself—was made of wood. Piles of logs and sawn boards sat about, too. Guarding against fire was an everyday habit for her family and the workers. Barrels full of water stood near the door to every workshop, with buckets ready to quickly douse any accidental blaze.

Now, though, she needed to think about *starting* a fire. "There are piles of wood shavings in the carpentry shops," Caroline said. "Those will catch fire easily.

Shall I gather some?"

Mama nodded. "That will do nicely."

Caroline ran to the nearest shop. The floor was littered with tiny curls of wood, left when the carpenters had carefully shaved pieces of wood to the exact shape they needed. Caroline quickly swept some shavings into a pile and filled a pail with the delicate bits.

Back outside, Caroline scanned the yard. The main building stood near the road. An open area, wide enough that the men could work with the huge trees they cut and dragged to the yard, stretched between the building and the half-built gunboat. Wooden support beams held the gunboat in place, pointed at the harbor so that it would be ready to slide into the water when it was finished. Small storage sheds squatted near the dock close by.

Where should they build the fire? The rain would make tending it difficult. Caroline decided on an open-air shelter where the carpenters sometimes worked, near the main building. The roof, held up by four tall posts, would help keep the firewood dry. From that spot, it would be easy to set fire to the sheds and the main building. After that, she and Mama could quickly run across the yard and set the gunboat on fire.

Caroline dumped the wood shavings in a pile beneath the shelter. Then she ran back to the shop and fetched an armful of bigger pieces of wood—stray chunks the men had tossed into one corner. She carried them to the shelter. Mama dragged over some boards.

When Caroline and Mama had gathered a good supply of wood, they built the fire, arranging kindling around a pile of shavings. Mama lit the shavings. Caroline carefully blew on them until the flames grew tall enough to catch the kindling. Soon the fire was snapping and crackling, bright against the deepening shadows.

"Well done," Mama said.

Caroline sat back on her heels and looked toward the navy shipyard. She could see a bonfire burning there, too. Its flickering glow was comforting, in a way. It reminded her that at least a few navy men were standing guard nearby. Caroline just hoped that the bonfires would not have to be used for anything more than keeping them warm that night.

"What else?" she asked Mama.

"Let's gather more wood shavings and scatter them

about the workshops, the office, and the sheds," Mama said. "If we do have to burn the yard, we'll want everything to catch fire quickly."

Caroline clenched her teeth as she walked through the familiar rooms, helping to prepare them for destruction. *This feels like a bad dream!* she thought. If only she could wake up and snuggle with her cat, Inkpot, and tell him all about the nightmare she'd had of burning Abbott's.

Finally, only the torches were left to prepare. Full darkness had settled over Sackets Harbor. Mama lit two lanterns and handed one to Caroline. "I'll find two stout sticks," Mama said. "Would you fetch some cloth, some twine, and the extra lamp oil?"

Caroline carried the lantern with great care as she walked through the sail loft to fetch cloth and went into the office to fetch twine and lamp oil. With wood shavings scattered about everywhere, she knew that if she stumbled and dropped the lantern, she might start a fire by accident.

She joined Mama at the bonfire. Mama handed her a long, heavy pole. She held it still while Mama wrapped cloth around one end and tied it in place with the twine. Then they prepared the second torch.

"Now, let's step well away from the fire," Mama said. Caroline caught a sharp whiff of lamp oil as Mama soaked the cloth. Caroline knew that after being drenched with the oil, the torch would need only a spark to catch fire. Once the torches were prepared, Mama laid them on bare ground a safe distance from the blaze.

Caroline scanned the shipyard, trying to steady herself. *If I must help burn the yard, I'll start with the skiff shed,* she thought. Since she'd sunk *Sparrow* to save Irish Jack's supply boat, the shed was empty.

With preparations complete, Caroline and Mama shared some of the food Grandmother had sent. Then Caroline helped Mama make a rough bed in the office. "One of us can sleep while one stands watch," Mama said.

"You can rest first, Mama," Caroline offered. She was tired, but she felt too jittery to sleep right away.

Mama nodded. "Very well. Be sure to tend the fire regularly. If you see or hear anything in the yard, come inside and wake me at once!"

Caroline crept out to the bonfire, found a log to sit on, and settled down to watch. The air was cold and damp. Raindrops dripped from the shelter roof. The shipyard was cloaked in darkness. She reminded herself that American soldiers and volunteers, including Papa, would do their best to keep the British away from Abbott's and the navy shipyard. But if they failed, and the British broke through . . . Caroline rubbed her eyes, trying to clear the picture of Abbott's in flames from her imagination.

A sudden rustle nearby made her jump. *That was likely just a mouse*, Caroline thought. Still, she added another chunk of wood to the fire. She welcomed its light.

Shivering, Caroline pulled her cloak tightly around her. Waiting all day for the British attack had been almost unbearable, but waiting at night was even worse. She had nothing to do but stare out at the dark yard, alone with her thoughts. Where was Papa right now? Was he trying to sleep on the cold ground, or perhaps keeping watch as she was? Did he have any notion that his precious shipyard might be destroyed by the time the battle ended?

Caroline tried to rub away the goose bumps on her arms. It was going to be a long night.

Caroline kept watch until she felt ready to sleep. Then she went inside, woke Mama, and curled up on the blanket.

She felt as if she'd barely drifted off to sleep when Mama touched her shoulder. "Your turn," Mama said.

Caroline yawned as she stumbled to her feet and headed back outside. The night had grown colder, and the damp air seeped through her cloak. Once she was perched on the log by the bonfire, she sat staring into the darkness beyond the shadows cast by the flames. *I must stay alert,* she reminded herself. If only her eyes didn't feel so sandy. If only she had something to do besides sit and think. Except for the crackling fire, everything seemed quiet—

Caroline jerked upright as a shadow moved across the yard, near the gunboat. She strained to see against the darkness. Yes! There it was again. Her heart suddenly seemed to beat much too fast.

She jumped to her feet and silently scurried back to the office. She eased the door open and slipped inside. "Mama, someone's out there!" she hissed.

Her mother scrambled to her feet. As she and

Caroline peered out the window, a second shadowy figure darted through the yard. He was visible in the fire glow for a moment, then gone.

Mama stepped to the door and cracked it open again. Caroline saw the silhouette of the pistol in Mama's hand. "Who's there?" Mama demanded in a terrible voice.

There was no answer.

"I'm a good shot," Mama warned. Caroline held her breath. Would Mama have to use the pistol?

A man's voice came from the yard. "We mean no harm."

"Be on your way!" Mama ordered.

The same voice spoke. "We're just two soldiers looking for a dry spot to sleep—"

Mama raised her hand and fired at the sky. Caroline jumped.

"You won't find your rest here tonight," Mama told the men. "Be on your way. Next time I won't aim for the clouds."

Through the window, Caroline saw two shadows dart back through the yard, heading toward the road. Mama waited for several more moments before closing the door again. "They've gone," she reported. She leaned against the closed door.

Caroline's heartbeat began to slow. "Why did you scare those men away?" she asked. "It's a cold, wet night, and if all they wanted was shelter . . ."

"If those men are American soldiers, they belong with their comrades," Mama said. "But what if they were thieves, or British spies? I'll have no strangers sneaking through our shipyard in the darkness."

Mama's right, Caroline thought. She took a deep breath and blew it out slowly. "It's a good thing Grandmother packed that pistol."

Mama reached out and squeezed Caroline's hand. "And a good thing you were willing to bring it."

Boom! Boom-boom!

Caroline jerked up from her blanket on the floor. Mama had taken the last watch, and now dawn was just beginning to lighten the day.

Boom-boom-boom!

"Oh!" Caroline gasped. Cannons were firing steadily, close enough and loud enough to make her rib cage quiver. The British must have landed! She pulled on her shoes and raced outside.

The rain had stopped. Mama stood by the bon-fire, arms crossed, listening. "Are we under attack?" Caroline cried. She lifted her face toward the sky. Wind shoved at her hair.

"The main British fleet must have landed—very close to town," Mama said.

Beneath the cannons' thunder, Caroline made out the rattle of muskets. The American men—*Papa!*—must be trying to fight off the British soldiers who'd landed.

"I'm going up to the sail loft," Mama said.

Caroline nodded. From the loft, it would be easier for Mama to see Navy Point, where—if needed—American men would send the signal to burn the shipyards.

Mama put her hands on Caroline's shoulders, as she had done the day before. "Keep the bonfire burn-ing. You may not be able to hear me call, so if I wave my arms at you, that will be your sign to light a torch and get to work."

"Yes, Mama," Caroline whispered. A shiver iced down her backbone, as if a bit of snow had slipped inside her collar.

"And I'll run down and destroy the gunboat," Mama said. "I saved some lamp oil to pour on the boat so that it will burn quickly. You set fire to the buildings."

Caroline took a deep breath. "I'll be ready."

"Remember, watch for my signal. God bless you, child. Stay safe." Mama kissed Caroline's forehead. Then she picked up her skirts and ran toward the sail loft.

Caroline decided to stand near the street, halfway between the main building and the gunboat. From there she could easily see the sail-loft window and could quickly grab a torch. She'd also be able to hear news from anyone passing by. Once she was in place, though, it was hard to stand still. Her skin tingled. Her hands trembled. She felt sick to her stomach.

This won't do, Caroline told herself sternly. It was too early to give up hope. Perhaps the American fighters would drive the enemy back before they came anywhere near the shipyard. Perhaps Mama would never have to give the signal to burn Abbott's. Caroline sent a silent message to Papa and the rest of the American men. *Hold strong. Don't let the British break through.*

Caroline left her post only to feed the bonfire from

time to time. As the day lightened, the battle noise grew louder, and Caroline saw a haze of gray smoke drifting into the western sky. There was no signal from Mama, though. Keeping her eye on Mama at the sail-loft window, Caroline paced anxiously back and forth.

A man on horseback galloped down the street toward the fighting, racing so fast that the animal's hooves sprayed mud behind them. Then several men in army uniform ran down the road in the opposite direction. Some carried guns. Some did not.

"Please—wait!" Caroline called after them. "What's happening?"

Two of the men kept running. The third paused. "God save us, girl, what are you doing here?"

Caroline quickly glanced up at Mama in the window. No signal yet. "Tell me what's *happening*," she begged.

A few more men ran past the yard. The soldier ran a hand over his grimy face. "We're in retreat!"

Caroline grabbed his sleeve. "Where are the militiamen?"

"They're running too!"

An icy hand seemed to clutch Caroline's heart as

she realized that the men running down the village's main street were fleeing from the British. "Is the battle lost, then?" she cried.

Instead of answering, the soldier pulled free and ran after his comrades.

In retreat. The words clanged in Caroline's mind like a bell. If the Americans were retreating, there might soon be no soldiers standing between the British and the shipyards. The signal to burn Abbott's could come at any moment.

A stray cannonball shrieked overhead. Caroline dropped to a crouch, crooking her arms over her head for protection. *Crash!* She peeked up just in time to see the chimney on a nearby warehouse explode. Caroline screamed, but she hardly heard her own voice. The cannonball sent chimney bricks tumbling like a child's blocks.

"Caroline? *Caroline!*" It was her mother's voice, faint beneath the sounds of battle. Caroline raised her head and saw Mama standing at the open window with one hand pressed against her heart.

Caroline got gingerly to her feet. She was shaking, but she managed a little wave in her mother's direction.

"I'm not hurt!" she yelled. From the window, Mama nodded.

The drifting smoke stung Caroline's eyes. Her ears ached from the deafening gunfire growing ever louder, ever closer. Beneath the roar, she heard shouts, a horse's wild whinny, crashes of timber and brick as another cannonball strayed into the village. More soldiers were running past the shipyard now, shouting and shoving, desperate to get away from the British.

"Stay steady," she ordered herself. She forced herself to stand and wait for the terrible order to burn the shipyard. It was the hardest thing she had ever done. Her knees trembled with longing to race after the fleeing soldiers. *I will not run*, Caroline told herself fiercely. *I will not abandon Mama. I will do whatever I must.* She repeated those words in her mind over and over.

Suddenly she heard Mama's voice again. Caroline looked up and saw Mama waving both arms frantically. "Go, Caroline!" Mama yelled. "It's time!"

Caroline ran and grabbed one of the torches. She needed both hands to control the heavy stick as she carefully tipped the end toward the bonfire. The oil-soaked cloth flared up at once.

With her heart thumping wildly, Caroline lifted the blazing stick and hurried to the skiff shed. She was clutching the torch so tightly that her fingers ached. Through the drifting smoke, she saw Mama run into the yard.

Caroline started to lower the torch toward the shavings and wood scraps she'd scattered against the shed walls the night before. Suddenly she thought of the joy in Papa's face when he'd returned to their ship-yard after his long months away. Her arms froze, and tears brimmed in her eyes. *I can't do it!* she thought.

Then, in the midst of the noise and commotion, Caroline heard Mama's voice in her memory: *We must not let Abbott's fall into enemy hands!*

In her heart, Caroline knew that, hard as it was, she had to carry out the plan. Tears ran down her cheeks as she lowered the blazing torch to the wood scraps. "I'm sorry, Papa," she whispered.

The shavings caught quickly. Flames darted out in both directions, licking greedily at the wood. The fire raced around the shed, gaining height and speed. Soon the front wall was burning.

Caroline turned away. Through tears and smoke,

she saw Mama splashing lamp oil against the gunboat's hull. Beyond her, across the harbor, black smoke billowed into the sky above Navy Point. The Americans had begun to burn their storehouses.

You must keep at it, Caroline told herself. She hurried to the nearest workshop. She dipped her torch, lighting wood shavings that she'd earlier piled against the wall.

"*Wait!*" someone bellowed.

Caroline looked up and saw Corporal Meyers running into the yard, waving his arms. "Stop!" he yelled. Chest heaving, he struggled to get the words out. "The storehouses—were set afire—by mistake!"

"But the Americans are retreating!" Caroline said. "I saw them running away."

"A few stood firm," Corporal Meyers told her. "And they saved the day."

Caroline's heart took a hopeful leap.

Corporal Meyers grinned. "Now it's the *British* who've turned tail! They're retreating back to Kingston!"

Caroline hurled her torch into the bonfire. She snatched her skirt high, away from the flames already beginning to flicker against the walls of the workshop.

Then she grabbed a wooden bucket, dunked it into
the nearby barrel, and poured water onto the flames.
Corporal Meyers ran to help. With a few more bucket-
fuls, the fire was out and the shop was safe.

Gasping for breath, Caroline looked over the rest
of the shipyard. The skiff shed's walls and roof were
in flames, sending a plume of black smoke skyward.
The shed stood apart from the other buildings, though.
Caroline didn't think the fire would spread.

Mama stood like a statue by the gunboat, still
holding her flaming torch. Caroline raced to join her.
She could see the dark damp splotches on the gunboat
where Mama had splashed the lamp oil.

"Heaven be praised," Mama whispered. "One more
moment, and I would have . . ." Her voice trailed away,
as if she couldn't bear to put her thought into words.

Caroline pulled the torch from her mother's hands,
ran across the yard, and threw it onto the bonfire.
As she rejoined her mother, she spread her arms wide
and twirled in a circle. "The shipyard is safe," she said
joyfully. "Oh, Mama, our shipyard is safe!"

Reunion

A moment later, Corporal Meyers joined Caroline and Mama. "The battle is won," he declared, his eyes dark with emotion. "And the British did *not* get what they came for." He put a hand on the gunboat, and then he looked toward the navy shipyard, where the mighty frigate still stood proud and tall, almost ready to launch.

Relief made Caroline feel light inside. She reached up and patted the gunboat too.

"Ladies, I salute you," the corporal said. "And now, I must return to my post." With a nod, he hurried from the shipyard.

"Let's send a message home to Grandmother," Mama said, wiping her eyes with the back of one hand. "I suspect our work is not yet over. We must stay here until we are relieved."

It didn't take Caroline long to understand what Mama meant. Some of the American militiamen were in wild spirits as they celebrated their victory. Twice, Mama had to order several rowdy men away from the shipyard.

All morning Caroline stayed by the Abbott's sign at the street, searching for Papa's face among the crowds of returning men as they walked past. At midday, Mr. Tate and several of the workers straggled back to the yard. They were filthy, and one had a cut on his shoulder where a musket ball had grazed him—but all were accounted for.

"None of our men was seriously hurt," Mr. Tate reported. "I told those who have families to go home."

"Have you seen Papa?" Caroline asked anxiously.

Mr. Tate shook his head. "I'm sorry, we have not, Miss Caroline. I expect he'll be along soon."

The workers began cleaning up the yard. Mama joined Caroline by the Abbott's sign, watching. The afternoon inched by. The street was crowded with returning soldiers, and Caroline's eyes ached from searching for her father's face. *I didn't lose hope when*

Papa was a British prisoner, she told herself. *I won't lose hope now.*

And then finally, *finally*, there he was. Caroline caught her breath when she spotted her father limping toward them. "Papa!" she shrieked.

Papa's face was grimy, and his eyes were bloodshot from smoke and exhaustion. But when he saw Caroline and Mama, he ran to them and swept them into a fierce hug.

Caroline clutched him so hard that her arms ached. She sent up a silent prayer of thanks for his safe return.

Then Mama led him gently to a nearby bench. The Abbotts settled together, Caroline snuggled close on one side of Papa and Mama on the other. "I've never been so glad to see you both," Papa said.

"We're fine," Caroline assured him.

"And we held the British off, by God," Papa murmured. "We held them off!"

Caroline pressed her cheek into his shoulder. Her heart was ready to burst.

After a moment, Papa asked, "What are you two doing here at the yard?"

Mama drew a deep breath. "Mr. Tate and the workers were called away to help fight the British," she told him. "Caroline and I couldn't leave the yard undefended."

Papa opened his mouth, then closed it again. Finally he said, "I can only imagine how difficult that must have been. I am proud of you both." After a moment he added quietly, "I heard that orders were given to burn the shipyards if need be." Papa looked slowly around the yard. Caroline wondered if he was imagining Abbott's in flames, just as she had.

Mama shuddered. "Fortunately, we heard the good news about the British retreat just in time. We had already lit our torches—"

"Oh, Papa, it was *awful!*" Caroline burst out. "I didn't think I could burn our yard. But I—I knew we couldn't let the British have it." She looked up at him. "Did we . . . do you think it would have been right to burn the yard?"

Papa wiped a hand over his face, which did nothing to improve his appearance. "You and Mama were faced with a dreadful situation, and you made the best decisions anyone could have." He squeezed their shoulders. "And in the end, nothing was lost."

That's not quite true, Caroline thought. She glanced toward all that was left of the skiff shed—ashes and blackened bits of wood. She knew she would never forget how it had felt to lower that torch and light the blaze. "One shed was lost," she said. "I set it on fire before we learned that the British were retreating. I'm sorry, Papa."

To her amazement, Papa laughed. "My dear daughter, the shed doesn't matter! My workers are safe. My business, and the gunboat, are safe. Best of all, my family is safe and together again."

Caroline nodded and let the last of her worries blow away like ash on the breeze.

Two weeks later, Caroline stood on the spot in Abbott's Shipyard where the skiff shed had once been. Grandmother had come to the yard, and so had the Hathaways and many of the Abbotts' friends and neighbors. The new gunboat was about to be launched!

It was a fine day for a celebration. Sunlight sparkled on Lake Ontario. A cool breeze kicked up little white-caps on the water. The air smelled of tar and turpentine and the grease that workers were spreading on wooden tracks that would guide the boat into the lake. Caroline sniffed the air happily. Nothing, she thought, smelled quite so fine as a shipyard on the day of a boat launch!

Rhonda nudged Caroline with her elbow. "This is exciting!" she exclaimed. "I've never seen a gunboat launched before."

"Nor have I," Rhonda's father, Lieutenant Hathaway, chimed in. He had returned with most of the American expedition force the day after the Battle of Sackets Harbor. "Although I do know firsthand how valuable gunboats are. We can't win this war without them."

Caroline grinned. "Oh, look! The men are ready."

The shipyard workers took up places on both sides of the gunboat, which sat at the top of the tracks. Each man held a big mallet. Papa walked briskly among them, checking to make sure that all was in place. "Ready!" he yelled. "Now!"

The shipyard workers raised their mallets and struck at the wedges holding the ship steady. *Thump! Thump! Thump!* The wedges fell away. The gunboat began to slide down the greased wooden tracks. Caroline stood on tiptoe, holding her breath.

"There she goes!" Papa called. The gunboat splashed

into the harbor, throwing up waves. Caroline laughed as she felt the spray on her face.

Rhonda jumped backward, clapping her hands. The workers whooped and hollered. The crowd cheered. Grandmother, who was seated nearby, gave Caroline a knowing nod. *You helped do this,* Grandmother's look said. *You helped defend this gunboat, which will now help defend us.*

Caroline's heart overflowed with pride. Soon the gunboat would be ready to strike at the British.

Mama tucked one hand through Papa's arm. Then she looked at Caroline and beckoned. Caroline joined her parents. "It's a fine gunboat," she told them.

"It is," Papa agreed. He smiled.

Caroline gazed out at the gunboat floating in the harbor, not far from the navy's enormous new frigate. *We showed the British that they don't control Lake Ontario,* she thought, standing straight and tall. *And if they come back, we'll beat them again.*

She knew that the war would surely bring more hardships and difficult choices. Right this moment, though, Caroline felt ready to face whatever might come.

Uncle Aaron's Letter

❧CHAPTER 11❧

June 1813

erow!

"Hush, Inkpot," Caroline murmured. She'd been dreaming about sailing Lake Ontario with Papa. A breeze kept them flying over the waves. Sunshine glistened on the water. Caroline didn't want to wake up.

The cat pawed her cheek. *Merow!*

Caroline sat up in bed, rubbing her eyes. Inkpot clearly had important business elsewhere. Caroline didn't know how long she'd been asleep, but the room was dark. She scooped the cat into her arms.

"Do you need to go outside?" Caroline whispered. Inkpot nudged her chin. *I'd better take you downstairs,* she thought. She didn't want the cat to wake anyone.

The night was pleasant, warm but not hot. Caroline padded silently down the steps. Her eyes were adjusting

to the darkness, so she had no trouble making her way
to the front door.

"Catch lots of mice!" she whispered. When she
cracked the door open, Inkpot bounded into the
night.

As Caroline turned back, she noticed a faint glow
coming from the parlor. She peeked inside. Papa sat
at the writing table in the far corner, studying some
papers by the light of a single candle.

"Papa?" she called softly. Having him home these
past weeks had been wonderful. After missing him for
so many months, Caroline didn't think she would *ever*
catch up on time spent with him.

Papa blinked and looked up, clearly startled. Then
he smiled. "Caroline! What are you doing up at this
hour?" He held out one hand with a look that said,
Please, come join me.

Caroline pattered across the floor and leaned against
him. "Inkpot wanted to go outside," she explained.
"What are *you* doing up?"

"I couldn't sleep," he told her. "So I . . ." He gestured
toward the papers.

Caroline saw that he'd been sketching a sloop.

"Oh, Papa! It's a *beautiful* ship." Her father was the best shipbuilder in all of New York, as far as she was concerned.

"I had many ideas for new designs while I was a prisoner," Papa said, "but no paper or pencil."

Caroline took a closer look at the sketches. Abbott's Shipyard was making gunboats for the American navy now, but she was glad to see that Papa was still thinking about the pretty merchant ships he loved to design. The British had stolen the last sloop her father had built, a sweet ship called *White Gull*. And now she and Papa couldn't take even short trips on the water because she'd destroyed his little skiff, *Sparrow*, to save Irish Jack's supply boat. "Oh, Papa," she said with a big sigh, "I wish we still had *Sparrow*. I do sorely miss sailing with you out on the lake!"

Papa squeezed her shoulder. "I miss that as well, daughter," he said. "One day we'll be able to sail clear across Lake Ontario again whenever we wish."

Caroline watched a moth flutter near the candle, then dance away. "I hope so," she said. "Sometimes it feels as if this war will never end."

"Don't lose faith." Papa's voice was low but firm.

"Soon we'll celebrate Independence Day. That will remind us that America has not been defeated!"

The reminder of Independence Day pushed away Caroline's gloomy thoughts. "I *am* excited about the celebration," she told him, bouncing on her toes. "Surely everyone in Sackets Harbor will gather! I've heard there will be music and speeches and a gun salute—even a concert by the navy musicians."

Papa smiled and then turned back to his drawing. Caroline felt very special, alone here with Papa while the rest of the house slept. It was a delicious treat to share this quiet time with him. She rested her head against his shoulder and studied his new design. With just a few pencil strokes, Papa had captured the sloop's graceful lines.

Caroline let her imagination wander back to the last time they'd sailed the lake together. She could almost hear timbers creaking and sails snapping in the wind. She could almost smell the fresh paint and damp breeze. She could almost feel the deck rocking gently beneath her feet. Her heart squeezed with longing to be back out on the water.

"Papa," Caroline whispered, "do you think you

might one day build a sloop for me?" She held her breath.

Papa was silent. Caroline wondered if he was remembering the last time she'd asked that question— right before they learned that their country was at war. "You're too flighty, Caroline," he'd told her that day. And, "If you want to sail on the Great Lakes, you must stay *steady*."

Now she added, "I've tried to be steady, Papa. I've tried to help Mama and Grandmother, and help at the shipyard, and . . ." Her voice trailed away. The last year had been so hard! She had made some mistakes, but she had also tried to prove to her family and friends that they could depend on her.

Papa touched her cheek. "My little Caroline," he said softly. "You're becoming such a fine young lady."

Caroline felt her hopes slide back toward her bare toes. *Fine young lady?* That was a nice compliment, but what she *wanted* to hear was Papa's assurance that he'd seen how steady and responsible she'd become while he was away.

Papa pulled her around to stand before his chair so that he could look at her directly. "It's very late, daughter." He leaned forward and kissed her forehead. "Go back to bed."

*I don't **want** to go back to bed*, Caroline thought. "But—" she began, before cutting the protest short. "Yes, Papa." She gave him a quick hug and left him alone with his own thoughts and dreams.

When Caroline woke, sun was streaming through the window. The scent of frying bacon drifted into the bedroom. She tossed the quilt aside and jumped to her feet. If she didn't hurry, she'd be late for breakfast.

A few moments later, Caroline skidded into the kitchen. She was glad to see her parents still at the table with Grandmother. Mama and Papa both worked at the shipyard now, and they often left home early.

"Gracious," Mama said. "Such a clatter!"

Grandmother added, "I thought that was a horse galloping down the stairs, not a young lady." Her eyes were merry, though. Caroline suspected that when Grandmother was a girl, she'd galloped down stairs sometimes, too.

Caroline swallowed a laugh before dutifully

saying, "I'm sorry." She took her place at the table. "May I go to the shipyard today?"

"It's baking day, Caroline," Grandmother reminded her.

"I meant, may I go to the shipyard after chores," Caroline said quickly. Baking was one of her least favorite activities, and usually their boarder, Mrs. Hathaway, helped Grandmother. Mrs. Hathaway had taken her daughters to visit relatives in Albany, however. Caroline knew she had to pitch in.

She was reaching for the milk jug when someone knocked on the front door.

"I'll get it," Mama said. She rose and wiped her hands on her apron before hurrying from the room. Caroline heard the murmur of voices in the hall. A moment later Mama returned, holding a folded piece of paper.

"What is it?" Papa asked.

"A letter from my brother Aaron," Mama replied. "His neighbor, Mr. Sinclair, brought it."

"Oh, good!" Caroline said. "I've been waiting to hear how Lydia likes the new farm." Uncle Aaron had recently purchased a farm several miles from

≥ Uncle Aaron's Letter ≥

Sackets Harbor, and Caroline knew that starting over would be a challenge for the Livingston family. When they'd fled Upper Canada the previous autumn, they'd had to leave behind their oxen and chickens and pigs, and many of their tools and household belongings.

Mama broke the circle of hardened wax that sealed the letter and began to read aloud.

My dear sister,

We recently received word that Martha's eldest sister is gravely ill. Martha packed a few things and left at once to tend to her.

As you know, starting a new farm here in New York has taken every penny we had. We used the last of our cash to buy a cow and her calf. Lydia is struggling to manage both the house and the cows while I work the fields.

"Oh, poor Lydia," Caroline said. She could well imagine how hard Lydia must be working.

The success of our new farm depends on making a good start this summer. We must have a good

harvest if we are to have any hope of surviving next
winter. Therefore, I ask that you send Caroline to
us right away. We will likely need her for some time
to come.

Caroline gasped. She was to go to the farm?
Right away? Without knowing when she might return?
A band seemed to go tight around her chest.

Mama pressed her lips together, as if she were
struggling too. Finally she finished reading the letter.

I write in haste, as my neighbors, Mr. and
Mrs. Sinclair, are eager to leave for Sackets Harbor.
They have promised to deliver this letter to you.
Their business in the village will take an hour or so,
no more. When they are finished, they will call upon
you again and escort Caroline to the farm. May
God keep you all.

> *Your brother,*
> *Aaron Livingston*

Caroline finally found her voice. "An hour? So
soon?" The last word came out as a squeak.

Mama and Papa shared a silent look. Then Mama slid next to Caroline and pulled her close. "Surely you will not hesitate," she said. "Lydia would help us if the situation were reversed."

"I want to help," Caroline said. "It's just that . . ." She looked at her father.

"We'll miss you very much," Papa told her. "But I know you will be a great help on the farm."

Caroline struggled to find words. This was happening so fast! Papa had been home for only a few weeks. Now she was about to be taken away from him, and Mama, and Grandmother. And Inkpot.

Away from the lake, too, Caroline thought. Her cousin's new farm was well inland, miles away from the lakeshore. Far away from her dream of once again sailing over Lake Ontario's dancing waves.

Well, one thing was certain—complaining wouldn't help anything.

Caroline stood. "Excuse me," she said quietly. "I'd best go upstairs and pack."

Meeting Garnet

All too soon, the Sinclairs' farm wagon carried Caroline into the forest beyond Sackets Harbor. She answered questions politely, trying to pretend that she felt cheerful about the trip.

Finally Mrs. Sinclair asked kindly, "Are you getting tired, Caroline?"

"A little," Caroline admitted. She'd been clutching the wagon seat as they bucked and jounced over the rough road. Her hands ached, and she felt rattled all the way to her bones. *Traveling by water is so much nicer than traveling on land*, she thought.

Mr. Sinclair gave her an encouraging smile. "We're getting close to your uncle's farm."

Caroline's heart grew heavier with every moment that the horse plodded away from her family, away from Lake Ontario, away from *home*. She knew that

Mr. and Mrs. Sinclair were doing Uncle Aaron a favor by bringing her, though, and she didn't want to seem ungrateful. "It was kind of you to fetch me," she said.

"It was no trouble," Mrs. Sinclair assured her. "Everyone in these parts is neighborly, always glad to help someone out."

"Well, not everybody," Mr. Sinclair muttered.

Caroline frowned. Was Mr. Sinclair thinking about someone in particular?

Mrs. Sinclair patted Caroline's knee. "Our neighbors are good people, but we seem to have a troublemaker skulking about. One of my best laying hens disappeared from my coop last week. Our closest neighbor had rhubarb cut right out of her garden."

"It's this war." Mr. Sinclair sounded disgusted. "The thief might be a deserter who ran off from the army or navy and is hiding in the woods. Or perhaps a soldier is sneaking away from camp, looking for fresh food."

"We've had trouble like that in Sackets Harbor, too," Caroline told them. "The soldiers and sailors get tired of eating dried peas and salt pork, so they raid people's gardens." She had no sympathy for thieves. No matter how boring the soldiers' meals were, stealing was wrong!

"Let's talk of more pleasant things," Mrs. Sinclair said. "Caroline, Mr. Sinclair and I are having a picnic on Independence Day. You'll be able to meet everyone who lives in these parts."

"That sounds nice." Caroline tried to smile, but the news didn't lift her spirits. She wanted to be with her family on Independence Day! She turned her head so the Sinclairs wouldn't see that she was already homesick.

The passing view only reminded Caroline that she was traveling farther and farther from home. Instead of a bustling village, she saw only a few scattered farms in the woods. Instead of smelling Lake Ontario's damp tang, she inhaled the scent of road dust. Instead of feeling a cool breeze blowing in from open water, her skin prickled with sweat.

When the wagon passed little clearings in the forest, Caroline glimpsed people hanging laundry or hoeing weeds or chopping firewood. The settlers seemed isolated from their neighbors. *It would be easy for a thief to watch one of these little farms from the woods*, she thought, *just waiting for the chance to snatch something for his supper.* Caroline rubbed her arms, feeling chilled. Had thieves troubled Uncle Aaron and Lydia?

"Here we are," Mr. Sinclair said. He turned the horse into a narrow lane that led to a farmyard. "Whoa now, Bess."

Finally! Caroline gratefully unclenched her fingers from the seat.

Lydia ran from the cabin to meet the wagon. "Caroline!" she cried.

Caroline scrambled to the ground and hugged her cousin. "I've come to help."

"I'm *so* glad." Lydia stepped back and gestured widely with one arm. "Welcome to our farm."

Caroline looked around. The farm looked . . . well, ragged. The clearing was stubbled with rocks. The only buildings were a small log cabin and an animal shed. Corn and pumpkins grew in straggly patches in a field still full of stumps. Potatoes had been planted in fence corners. Caroline tried to hide her dismay. No wonder Uncle Aaron had sent for her! Any help she gave Lydia with gardening and household chores would let her uncle spend more time in the field.

"Papa was able to buy this farm for a low price because the previous owners cleared very little land before they moved on again," Lydia said. "I know it doesn't look like much—"

"But it will soon," Caroline said firmly.

Uncle Aaron hurried across the yard. "Thank you for coming, Caroline," he said. "Is your family well?"

"Yes," she told him. "They all send greetings."

Uncle Aaron thanked Mr. and Mrs. Sinclair for bringing Caroline. "I'll be by your place on Thursday to help cut your hay," he promised. He handed Mrs. Sinclair a little crock. "Here's some fresh butter— a gift from Minerva."

Caroline leaned close to Lydia and whispered, "Who is Minerva?"

Lydia waved good-bye to her neighbors before answering. "Our cow! Would you like to see her and the calf?"

"I would," Caroline told her.

Lydia led the way into the animal shed, where a cow stood in a square stall. "Oh, my!" Caroline gasped. She had sometimes seen whole herds of cows being driven through Sackets Harbor, but she'd never been so close to a cow before. Here inside this little shed, Minerva looked very big! She was reddish-brown—except for her long, curved horns, which were cream-colored.

I will have to stay away from those horns, Caroline thought.

Then the calf appeared from behind Minerva, walking on knobby legs. The calf was the same color as her mother. She had black eyes and long eyelashes. Caroline felt her heart melt like butter in the sun. "Oh, she's sweet," Caroline said. "What's her name?"

"She doesn't have one yet," Lydia told her. "Papa and I decided to let you name her."

"Truly?" Caroline asked. What an honor! She studied the calf thoughtfully. "Do you remember Grandmother's garnet ring—the one Grandfather gave her when they were courting? The calf is as red as the garnet stone. Let's call her that."

"I like that," Lydia said. "Garnet it shall be."

Caroline leaned over the stall railing. The little calf had captured her heart. "I think you and I are going to be friends," Caroline whispered to the calf. "Good friends indeed."

That afternoon Caroline helped Lydia heat water and scrub milk pans, buckets, and a butter churn. "Having a dairy cow is a lot of work," Lydia told her.

"When we finish washing these things, we'll put them away in the springhouse."

"Where is the springhouse?" Caroline asked.

Lydia handed her two tin milk pans to carry. "Come along. I'll show you."

The springhouse was built into the side of a hill in the woods behind the cowshed. It was so overgrown with blackberry brambles that Caroline barely saw the door before Lydia opened it. The springhouse was dim inside and smelled like damp earth. A shallow stream ran right through one corner, keeping the room cool. "This is like a hidden cave!" Caroline marveled as her eyes adjusted to the gloom.

"The springhouse was here when we bought the farm," Lydia said. "It's bigger than we need right now."

"Well," Caroline said, "perhaps one day you'll have a whole herd of cows."

"I like that idea." Lydia grinned. "It would keep me busy, though. See those wooden racks?" She pointed to one wall. "After I milk Minerva, I pour the fresh milk into these pans and put them on the racks to cool. When the cream rises to the top, I skim it off and save it until I have enough to churn into butter."

"Doesn't Garnet need all of Minerva's milk?" Caroline asked.

"I'm milking Minerva only once a day, so there's plenty left for Garnet," Lydia explained. "Besides, Minerva sometimes pushes Garnet away now. She knows her calf is old enough to start eating on her own. You and I must coax Garnet along, because I really need all of Minerva's milk! I can sell butter at the general store, or trade it for other supplies."

Caroline nodded. She'd never thought about how precious milk or butter could be.

"Sometimes I daydream about buying sugar and baking something sweet," Lydia said. "We haven't had a bit of sugar since we came here." Then she folded her arms, looking determined. "That's no matter, really. What *is* important is growing enough food this summer to last us through the winter. We're not eating much now but dried peas and beans. I'm so hungry for something different!"

I should have brought food with me, Caroline thought. At home, there were still dried apples and turnips and sweet potatoes in her family's root cellar, and more were available in the market stalls near the harbor.

She hadn't realized how hard it would be to find food on a new farm in early summer, when harvesttime for most crops was still many months away.

That evening the girls made a kettle of bean soup for supper. "You can see why we need your help," Uncle Aaron told Caroline as they settled at the table. "I need to work in the field, and Lydia can't manage Minerva, the garden, cooking, and household chores by herself. Caroline, I know you'll be a big help with chores. Will you also take charge of teaching Garnet to eat on her own? I'd like you to get her used to being led, too."

"I'm happy to!" Caroline assured him as she scooped up a spoonful of soup. Other than Inkpot, she'd never had the chance to take care of a baby animal before.

"We need your help with something else, too," Uncle Aaron said with a sigh. "Lately some of our neighbors have had eggs stolen from their chicken coops, and vegetables taken right from their gardens."

"The Sinclairs told me about that," Caroline said.

Lydia looked worried. "Yesterday I left a pail of milk sitting near the shed by mistake," she said. "When I went to fetch it later, the pail was gone."

Uncle Aaron leaned his forearms on the table and looked at Caroline. "We all must keep watch for anyone sneaking about our property. If you see anyone, fetch me at once."

"I will," Caroline promised. She hoped the thief would stay far away from their farm.

Uncle Aaron and Lydia were quiet. *They have more challenges than I even imagined,* Caroline thought. She looked around the little cabin—just one room and a loft. She and her parents had once lived in a log cabin, but she remembered it as a cheerful place, with pretty embroidered samplers on the wall and colorful woven coverlets on the beds. The Livingstons hadn't been able to take such treasures with them when they fled from Upper Canada. This cabin looked bare and lonely.

Caroline turned to her cousin. "Lydia, I brought some sewing supplies. Perhaps we can start making a quilt."

Lydia's face broke into a grateful smile. "Oh, I'd like that!"

That night, Caroline and Lydia settled down in the loft. Lydia fell asleep quickly, and Caroline soon heard her uncle snoring downstairs. She eased from the bed and tiptoed to the window. Nothing moved in the clearing below. The stumps in the field looked like strange, hunched creatures in the moonlight. She tried to get her bearings so that she could look toward Lake Ontario. Toward home. *I want to help Lydia and Uncle Aaron*, she thought. *But I wish their farm wasn't so far from Sackets Harbor.* Now, with everything silent and no chores or conversation to fill her hands and her mind, homesickness rushed back.

The best thing I can do is keep busy, Caroline reminded herself. That wouldn't be hard! Not with dairy chores, gardening, cooking, cleaning, sewing, and especially tending Minerva and Garnet.

Caroline nodded, feeling determined. With her help, Garnet would grow strong, the garden would produce lots of potatoes and onions and beans, and the Livingston farm would be a success.

A Big Mistake

I t's so nice to have you here," Lydia told Caroline as they walked to the cowshed the next morning. "I've been lonely since we left Sackets Harbor. I—" She stopped suddenly and stared toward the shed.

Caroline felt a flicker of alarm. "What's wrong?"

Lydia pointed to the shed door, which hung slightly open. "I'm sure I latched that last night."

"The cows!" Caroline cried. She flung the door open and ran inside, with Lydia right on her heels. She felt limp with relief when she saw Garnet and Minerva.

Lydia sagged against the wall. "Oh, thank heavens. Maybe I only *thought* I'd latched the door."

Or maybe, Caroline thought, *the thief has his eye on Garnet and Minerva*. Perhaps he'd intended to steal the cows, but something had scared him away first.

"I'll tell Papa later," Lydia said. "For now, let's see how our girls are doing."

Caroline and Lydia leaned on the stall railing, watching Garnet nurse hungrily from her mother. Minerva seemed impatient. Every few minutes she walked restlessly away from Garnet.

"See that?" Lydia asked. "Minerva wants Garnet to start eating on her own."

"What will Garnet eat now?" Caroline asked.

"This morning we'll start teaching her to drink milk from a bucket," Lydia said. "We'll gradually change that to water. She'll learn to eat hay and grass and vegetables, too." She fastened a rope halter around Minerva's head. "I'm going to take Minerva outside so Garnet can't nurse. You stand by the door and close it before Garnet can follow us."

Caroline hesitated. "What if Minerva pokes you with her horns?"

"Minerva is as gentle as a lamb," Lydia assured her. "Little Garnet is the one you have to watch out for!"

Lydia led Minerva out to a small pen behind the shed. When Caroline shut the door, Garnet bawled in protest.

Caroline gently patted Garnet. She liked how the calf's thick hair felt both soft and bristly. "Poor thing," Caroline told her. "I know just how you feel. I miss my mother, too."

Garnet turned her head. She seemed to be listening carefully.

"And silly Lydia told me I had to watch out for you," Caroline scoffed. By the time Lydia returned with a bucket of milk, Caroline and Garnet were getting along just fine.

"Time for Garnet's first lesson," Lydia said.

"May I try?" Caroline asked eagerly.

Lydia handed her the bucket. "Dip your fingers in the milk," she instructed.

Caroline put her fingers into the warm milk. "Now what?"

"Put your hand in front of Garnet's mouth and let her suck from your fingers," Lydia said. "Calves don't have upper teeth, so she can't hurt you."

"Want some milk?" Caroline asked, stretching her hand toward Garnet. She held her breath. The calf sniffed once before taking Caroline's fingers into her mouth. Garnet's tongue felt rough, and she sucked with

so much force that for a moment Caroline wasn't sure
she'd be able to get her fingers back! Once the milk was
gone, however, she was able to pull her hand away.

Garnet sucked milk from Caroline's fingers several
times. Each time, Caroline held her hand closer and
closer to the bucket.

"Now," Lydia said finally, "keep your fingers right
at the surface of the milk."

Caroline dipped her fingers back into the milk.
Garnet looked at her hand and snorted.

"Come now, Garnet," Caroline coaxed. "You can
do it."

Instead of putting her nose into the milk, Garnet
butted her head against the bucket—*hard*. Thrown
off balance, Caroline stumbled and couldn't stay on
her feet. She landed on her backside. A spray of milk
landed on her.

Lydia sputtered with laughter. "I told you she was
strong!"

Once Caroline was over her surprise, she laughed
too. She rose to her feet and dusted herself off. Bits
of straw clung to the back of her skirt, and milk and
cow drool streaked the front. "I thought Garnet was

ready to drink from the bucket! Why did she hit it?"

"She wasn't being mean," Lydia said. "She butts her head against Minerva when she wants milk. It's her way of saying she's hungry."

The calf gazed up at Caroline with her big, dark eyes as if to say, *I'm sorry you fell down.*

"You're a rascal," Caroline scolded her lightly. "Next time you want something, please be more polite!"

Once the girls had finished tending the cows and cleaning the stall, they tackled the huge vegetable garden. It was surrounded by a board fence so that rabbits and deer couldn't munch the produce. When Lydia opened the gate, it gave a loud screech.

"Gracious!" Caroline clapped her hands over her ears. She hurried inside and waited until Lydia closed the gate behind them—with another screech—before lowering her hands again.

"Papa was planning to fix that," Lydia said, "but now that a thief is about, Papa's glad the gate screeches. He says we'll hear anyone trying to sneak into *our* garden."

"I should say so," Caroline agreed.

Lydia looked at the garden and shook her head. "Mama and I planted lots of seeds, but look how many weeds have grown in! I can't even tell what vegetables have sprouted."

"Well," Caroline said briskly, "let's get started."

Caroline had often helped Grandmother in their garden, so she knew what to do. In the nearest row, small, lacy carrot plants had poked through the soil in a tidy line, but tall weeds were choking them. Caroline knelt and began pulling the weeds carefully, making sure that she didn't damage any of the carrots. She wondered if Grandmother was weeding the garden at home, all by herself. Was she managing?

I'm needed here, Caroline reminded herself. She took a moment to gently push thoughts of Sackets Harbor from her mind. Through her skirt, the earth felt warm against her knees. She heard the ringing blows of Uncle Aaron's ax as he hacked at a stump in the nearby field, and the contented buzz of a fat bumblebee drifting past, and Lydia's voice when she began to sing a hymn nearby.

Soon the wave of homesickness passed, and

Caroline finished weeding her row. "This looks much better," she said, sitting back on her heels and admiring the carrot plants. "Lydia, do you think we should stop for now?" The sun was high overhead.

Lydia wiped sweat from her cheek, leaving a smudge of dirt behind. "Papa will want his midday meal soon," she agreed. She pointed to a far corner of the garden. "There's some asparagus back there that might be ready to eat. Would you look and see? I've gathered some watercress and a few wild leeks this spring, but they don't taste nearly as good as the first bite of fresh asparagus!"

Caroline loved fresh asparagus too—the spring's first tender stalks were a treat after eating wrinkled beets and pickled cabbage all winter. She eagerly made her way to the asparagus patch, making sure not to step on any tiny vegetable plants. The garden's far corner was thick with tall weeds. Caroline pushed them aside, searching. Where was the asparagus? She didn't see any of the straight green spears poking from the earth. Finally she knelt and crawled back and forth, parting weeds with her hands.

Then she stopped short. "Oh no," she moaned.

No wonder she'd had trouble finding the asparagus! Every stalk had been sliced off, leaving just the barest nub of green above the soil. "Lydia? Come look at this."

Lydia joined her and stared at the asparagus nubs. "Someone *cut* those."

"I'm afraid so," Caroline said. "And stole every last stalk."

"But how did the thief get into the garden without Papa or me hearing?" Lydia put her hands on her hips, staring at the noisy gate.

Caroline scanned the garden, trying to find an answer. "I suppose someone might have climbed over the fence," she said doubtfully, "but it would have been hard." The boards were tall and smooth.

Lydia stamped one foot. "First the thief took a pail of milk, and now this. I was counting on that asparagus! Just thinking about it made my mouth water." She glared at the damage for a moment. Then she sighed. "I'd better fetch Papa. He'll want to see this."

When Uncle Aaron saw the nubs, he muttered something under his breath.

"And there's more bad news," Caroline told him. "We found the shed door unlatched this morning, too."

Uncle Aaron rubbed his face with one hand. "We can't have any more thievery on our place," he said. "I'll have to start keeping watch at night."

"Oh, Papa," Lydia fretted. "You can't work hard all day and then sit up all night!"

He stared at the asparagus nubs grimly. "If the scoundrel stole vegetables, he might steal Minerva or Garnet next."

Caroline felt a hitch in her chest. Lydia and her father needed those cows. They'd spent the last of their money to buy them! Without those cows, the farm might fail. Besides . . . Caroline couldn't bear the thought of a thief leading those sweet animals away.

"I'll help keep watch," Caroline told her uncle.

"I will as well," Lydia said quickly.

Uncle Aaron put one arm around each girl's shoulders. "You need your sleep, but I will be glad for a bit of help. Don't fear. I'm sure the thief will be caught soon."

Yes, Caroline thought, *but how much more will he steal before that happens?*

❀

That evening, Caroline visited Garnet and Minerva in their pen behind the shed. "There, now," Caroline said soothingly as she approached the calf. "Uncle Aaron said you need to practice being led."

Garnet jumped sideways when Caroline reached for her rope halter. Caroline was glad that the cows were in the small pen, so Garnet didn't have much room to scamper away. Caroline tried again, moving her hand more slowly. This time she grasped the rope. "Good girl!" she said.

Garnet clearly wasn't sure that she wanted to be led, but Caroline managed to tug the calf in a circle around the pen. "You know, Garnet, this would be easier in a bigger space," Caroline said.

A single wooden rail served as a gate between the pen and a fenced pasture. Caroline considered the pasture, which was green and thick with grasses and other plants. "We'd have a lot more room out there."

She slid the rail out of the way and led Garnet through the opening. Minerva followed right behind. Once they were in the pasture, Caroline found it much easier to work with Garnet. Minerva contentedly munched tender green shoots, and Garnet followed

Caroline around the pasture with only a few dancing hops of protest.

As they walked, Caroline told Garnet about her own family. Then she described Sackets Harbor. "The lake is bigger and grander than you can imagine," she said. "I love sailing on the lake more than anything else."

Garnet tossed her head.

"Is that enough for now?" Caroline asked. "You've done very well. Let's lead your mama back into the shed, shall we?"

Caroline led Garnet back to the pen and on to the shed. "Come along, Minerva!" Caroline called.

Minerva, happily gobbling grass, ignored her.

This won't do, Caroline thought. She'd never tried to lead Minerva, but Lydia had said the cow was gentle. "I hope that's true," Caroline murmured, eyeing those long, curved horns. Moving very slowly, she approached Minerva and grasped the cow's halter. It took all of Caroline's strength to pull Minerva's head away from her meal. After that, though, the cow seemed willing to be led into the shed.

Caroline was proud of her accomplishment. She'd led both Garnet and Minerva by herself! "Sleep tight," she told the cows as she left them. "I'll help keep watch tonight so that you stay safe." No one was going to steal the Livingston cows if she could help it.

Caroline and Lydia each took a turn sitting up by the front door that night, watching and listening for the thief. There was no sign of trouble, thankfully, but it was a long night. As Caroline made cornmeal mush for breakfast the next morning, she couldn't stop yawning. Uncle Aaron had done most of the guard duty, though, and Caroline knew that he must be even more weary.

"I almost fell asleep while I was milking Minerva," Lydia confessed when she returned from the cowshed with pail in hand. "I put most of the milk in the spring-house to cool, but here's some for our breakfast. And I have a surprise." She proudly pulled three radishes from her pocket. "Fresh from our garden! At least the thief didn't get these."

Uncle Aaron smiled. "Our very first harvest!" He made a show of taking one of the radishes and crunching it between his teeth, closing his eyes while he ate. "I believe," he said, "that this is the finest radish ever grown."

Caroline dished up the cornmeal mush. "Are you going to the Sinclairs' today?" she asked her uncle.

He nodded. "His hay is ready to cut. I'm always happy to help out a neighbor. Mr. Sinclair promised to give me some of the hay in return, too."

Minerva will like that, Caroline thought. She took her place at the table and sleepily poured Uncle Aaron a cup of milk.

When he tasted it, he sputtered and choked and spit the milk back into his cup. "Oh!" he gasped, wiping his mouth with his hand. "That tastes awful!"

Lydia grabbed the milk pitcher and sniffed. "It doesn't smell good, either."

"Minerva must have eaten something she shouldn't have." Uncle Aaron looked confused. "But how could that be? We've been so careful to keep her in the pen!"

Caroline's cheeks grew hot. *Oh **no**,* she thought.

"I can't imagine," Lydia was saying.

"I can," Caroline said in a small voice. "Yesterday evening, when you were both busy, I . . . I took the cows into the pasture behind their little pen."

Lydia looked dismayed. "That pasture is full of wild leeks! Minerva must have eaten some. That's what spoiled her milk."

"I'm very sorry." Caroline looked from her cousin to her uncle. "I just wanted more room to practice leading Garnet. I didn't know about the leeks!"

Lydia sighed. "I haven't had time to dig them out yet. I should have told you."

Caroline pleated her skirt between her fingers. "How long will Minerva's milk be spoiled?"

"It will taste like onions for several days, probably," Lydia said.

Caroline had often gathered wild leeks in the spring so that Grandmother could cook with them. Caroline liked their oniony taste in soups and stews. But in milk? No.

Then a new thought filled her with panic. "What about Garnet? Will she stop nursing?"

Lydia shook her head. "When she's hungry enough, she'll eat. I'll have to throw the rest of the milk away, though."

Caroline stared at her hands. She'd only wanted to help! Now Lydia wouldn't have milk to churn into butter—butter that she could have sold or traded for something she needed.

"Don't worry, we'll get by," Lydia said. Then she snickered. "And—oh, Papa! I wish you could have seen the look on your face when you tasted that milk!"

"Now, Lydia. Don't be unkind to your father," Uncle Aaron said, chuckling.

Caroline was grateful for their laughter, but she wasn't able to join in. *No more mistakes!* she told herself. On the Livingston farm, every bit of food was too valuable to waste.

All Alone at the Farm

After breakfast, Uncle Aaron left to help the Sinclairs. Caroline and Lydia began washing dishes. Caroline tried to think of a way to make up for her mistake. Radishes and cornmeal mush—with no milk—made a poor meal for a farmer.

"Lydia," she asked, "are there any creeks nearby? Perhaps we could catch some fish and surprise your papa with a fine dinner."

Lydia grinned. "Oh, he'd love that," she said. "There's a good stream that's not too far away. I'd better stay here to keep an eye on things, but you could go."

Caroline had hoped that she and Lydia could go fishing together. That would be much more fun! *But what's most important is helping her and Uncle Aaron,* Caroline reminded herself. "I'll go," she promised. "First, let's get a bit more work done in the garden."

By mid-morning, Caroline had planted melon seeds and cleared the cucumber and onion patches of weeds. Lydia was carefully digging up little cabbage seedlings that had crowded too close together and replanting them where they had more room to grow. As Caroline watched her cousin work, she felt a fresh wave of anger toward the thief. Her cousin, and Uncle Aaron and Aunt Martha too, were working very hard to make this farm a success. How dare someone sneak into the garden and take what didn't belong to him?

A rustle nearby caught Caroline's attention. A chipmunk, its cheeks bulging, darted past and disappeared among some weeds by the fence. "Did you eat my melon seeds?" Caroline demanded. "Those were not for you!" She crawled after him, staying close to the ground. If she could find the chipmunk's hole in the garden fence, she'd try to plug it.

"What are you doing?" Lydia called.

Caroline tugged at a big weed next to the fence. "A chipmunk stole some of the melon seeds! There must be a little tunnel under the fence, or a gap between two boards."

"If you find a hole, fill it in," Lydia said. "I don't

want so much as a baby mouse in here."

Caroline searched among the weeds along the fence until she found a knothole near the bottom of one board, big enough to make a nice doorway for mice or chipmunks. She gathered a few stones to block the hole. When she tried to do that, however, she got a surprise. The board moved!

Frowning, Caroline studied it more carefully. The top nail holding the board was still in place, but the bottom nail was missing. Caroline was able to swing the plank back and forth like the pendulum on a mantel clock.

"My goodness!" she said. "Lydia, come and see!"

Lydia patted another cabbage into the dirt before joining Caroline. "I didn't know we had a loose board," she said. "Papa can fix that."

"Do you suppose the thief might have crawled into the garden through this gap?" Caroline asked.

Lydia tipped her head, considering. "It's awfully narrow."

Caroline squinted at the plank. *Could* someone squeeze through that opening? There was one way to find out. She pushed the plank to one side and began wriggling through. "Ooh!" she gasped as the unmoving boards on either side of the opening scraped against her arms. In a moment, though, she was on the far side of the fence.

"If the thief did come through here," she said, "he must be skinny."

"Very skinny indeed." Lydia's voice was still doubtful. "I'm afraid to try it. Wait a moment." Lydia disappeared, and Caroline heard the gate screech open and then screech closed again before her cousin joined her outside the fence.

Lydia frowned, looking from the nearby woods to the loose board. "It wouldn't be hard for a thief to watch from the forest until it was safe to sneak into the garden."

As Caroline considered the gap in the fence, something caught her eye. She pointed to a single red thread snagged on one of the boards beside the loose one. "Look at this!"

Lydia crouched beside her. "I don't own any red clothes," she said. "Papa doesn't either."

"The thread must have come from the thief," Caroline said. "It hasn't been there long enough to fade in the sun. The color is still bright."

"So the thief is very skinny and was wearing some-thing red." Lydia shook her head. "I don't know how that helps us."

"With a better idea of what to look for," Caroline said, "maybe we can find him!"

When Caroline was ready to go fishing, Lydia gave her directions. "Walk to the southwest corner of the field." She pointed. "From there, follow the path down-hill through the woods. It will take you to the stream."

"I won't get lost," Caroline assured her.

"If you catch some fish, it will be a wonderful treat for Papa," Lydia said. "It will be fun to surprise him."

As she set out, Caroline realized that she didn't really mind heading to the creek on her own. She'd brought a fishing pole and a moss-lined basket to carry her catch. Stuffed into her pocket was an old tobacco tin holding worms and grasshoppers. Fish could be choosy. She liked having two kinds of bait.

I'll pretend I'm on a treasure hunt, she thought. Catching some fish to surprise Uncle Aaron would be almost as good as finding a gold piece! And with luck, she'd be able to bring back a treat for Lydia, too.

A short way down the trail, Caroline spotted a huge sycamore tree, dead for so long that the trunk was hollow. Had honeybees started a hive inside the trunk? Honey would be a wonderful treat for her cousin. Caroline held her breath and tiptoed closer, watching for bees, listening for the telltale buzzing. The trunk was silent and empty, however.

Caroline returned to the path. Soon she saw some sweet william flowers. *I'll pick those for Lydia on my way back,* she decided. The pretty pink blossoms would brighten the dark cabin.

Before too long, Caroline reached the stream. The water was clear and fast, tumbling over rocks, gurgling past banks shaded with willows. *This stream must flow to Lake Ontario,* she thought with a stab of homesickness. She paused, trying to imagine herself back in Sackets Harbor. What was happening at the shipyard? Was Papa still working on his design for a new sloop? She could almost hear gulls calling and waves slapping at the ship . . .

A woodpecker banged loudly on a nearby tree,

startling Caroline from her daydream. "You're here to fish," she reminded herself. "Get busy."

Before trying her luck, she made her way downstream. Sometimes the biggest fish lurked in still pools along the bank. After shoving through the underbrush for a few moments, she spotted just such a pool. "Perfect!" she announced.

Then she saw something else. Someone had stretched a piece of cotton cord over the creek, tying each end to the trunk of a small tree. Several shorter strings had been tied to the cord and dangled into the water. Caroline could see wire hooks dancing just below the surface. None had snagged a fish.

Her pleasure in the fine day vanished as quickly as a cloud might cross over the sun. Who had left these fishing lines? Was this still Uncle Aaron's land, or was it someone else's property? Caroline wasn't used to worrying about such things. Back home, good fishing spots were so plentiful that anyone could easily find a quiet place to enjoy.

But Caroline wasn't in Sackets Harbor anymore. She didn't know how things were done around here. And she didn't know who was sneaking about at night, stealing from honest folk.

Caroline told herself that the person who had set these fishing lines was most likely a neighbor. And yet, if the thief was an army deserter, hiding in the woods . . . well, someone like that might very well try to catch fish in this lonely spot.

Caroline turned in a circle, studying the woods uneasily. She saw no sign of anyone, but she decided not to stay so close to the fishing rig. She followed the stream back to the spot where she'd left the trail.

She still felt nervous. *Perhaps I should go back to the cabin,* she thought. But she'd come here to fish! She forced herself to bait her hook.

By the time shadows stretched long, she'd caught two speckled brook trout. Caroline hesitated. She had hoped to catch more than that! But she couldn't stop wondering if someone might be watching her from behind a nearby tree.

This will do for today, she decided. She dampened the moss in her basket to keep the fish cool. Then she headed for the cabin.

When Caroline got back to the farm, she told Lydia about the fishing rig.

"A neighbor might have left it," Lydia said, "but it's hard to know."

Caroline tried to put her unease out of her mind. "I brought these flowers home for you," she said. Lydia's face glowed when she saw the pretty blossoms.

When Uncle Aaron returned just before dark, dusty and tired, he was delighted to find fried fish, cornbread, and a salad of tart dandelion greens waiting. "What a feast!" he exclaimed. "Thank you, girls."

Caroline felt warm inside. She'd come to help with chores, but it felt even better to cheer up her cousin and uncle.

"I thought we might share one fish tonight and save the other for tomorrow," Lydia told her father. "I put it in the springhouse to keep it from spoiling."

"Uncle Aaron, someone left a fishing line strung over the creek," Caroline said. "Do you think it might have been left by the thief?"

Uncle Aaron frowned slightly. "Perhaps. I don't recall ever seeing a rig like that around here."

For a moment, no one spoke. Caroline imagined

a runaway soldier creeping through the woods near the farm. The picture made her shiver.

"Will you need to help at the Sinclair place tomorrow?" Lydia asked her father.

"The job's not finished, so I will," Uncle Aaron replied. He forked up another small bite of trout, clearly savoring every morsel. "Mrs. Sinclair reminded me about her Independence Day picnic," he added. "It will be a fun day."

But not as fun as Independence Day in Sackets Harbor, Caroline thought wistfully.

"Lydia, Mrs. Sinclair asked if you'd be willing to come with me tomorrow," Uncle Aaron said. "She has half a dozen men to feed at midday, and she'd be glad of your help."

Caroline stopped eating. "What about me?" she asked.

"I wish we could take you as well," Uncle Aaron began, "but . . ."

"But someone must stay and watch for the thief," Caroline said. She swallowed hard. She didn't like the idea of being alone all day, but she tried not to show it. "I understand."

Uncle Aaron seemed to guess her feelings. "The thief has always struck at night," he reminded her. "There's no reason to think he would try to steal something in daylight."

Lydia clapped a hand over her mouth. "Oh! That reminds me. Caroline discovered something else today." She described the loose board and showed her father the red thread.

"I'll nail the loose board down right away," he said. He finished the water in his mug, wiped his mouth on his sleeve, and got to his feet. "If the scoundrel used that gap to slip into our garden, he'll be surprised if he comes back."

That night, when Caroline took her turn keeping watch by the front door, she reminded herself that the thief would have to use the screechy gate to reach the garden now. She sat on the front step in the darkness, feeling very alone, straining her eyes and her ears for any hint of an intruder. An owl hooted once, but that was all.

Maybe the thief has moved on, she thought. Since she'd be all alone on the farm the next day, she wanted to believe that he'd done just that.

Caroline waved good-bye to Uncle Aaron and Lydia when they set off for the Sinclair farm. Uncle Aaron carried a hay fork over one shoulder. "We'll be home as soon as we can," he promised.

"Don't worry," Caroline said stoutly. "I'll be fine." Still, once they'd disappeared down the lane, she felt lonely.

But I'm not truly alone, Caroline reminded herself. She still had Minerva and Garnet for company.

Lydia had left the cows in their shed. Caroline decided to visit them before washing the breakfast dishes. She felt better when Minerva turned her head and gave a low *moo-oo* of greeting. Caroline liked her warm cow smell, and the way Garnet peeked out from beneath her long, dark lashes as if she were too shy to say good morning.

"Garnet," Caroline said, "may I lead you around your pen a few times? It will be good practice."

Garnet gave a little sideways prance.

Caroline laughed. "That must mean you're ready to go." She was able to grab the calf's halter easily this time. "Good girl," she crooned as she led Garnet to the door.

Caroline was about to step outside when a sudden spot of color caught her eye. Something red flashed in the trees on the far side of the clearing. Caroline stood still as stone, peeping around the door frame. There it was again! Something was moving through the underbrush—something as red as a cardinal, but bigger.

Was it someone wearing a shirt as red as the thread she'd found on the garden fence?

Caroline jumped back into the dim shed, heart pounding. Uncle Aaron was gone. Lydia was gone. Had the thief watched them leave? Was he prowling around the farm believing that no one was home?

What should I do? Caroline thought desperately. Her first impulse was to run into the cabin, latch the door, and stay there until Uncle Aaron and Lydia got home.

Garnet bumped her nose against Caroline's hip. She seemed to be saying, *What about me?* Caroline swallowed. She couldn't simply hide in the cabin and leave the garden and the cows to the thief.

I could hide the cows in the woods, Caroline thought. If she did that, the garden would be left unprotected.

But if she stood watch in the garden and left Minerva and Garnet here, the thief might steal them both!

Whatever she did, Caroline knew she had to act fast. *It would be easier for Uncle Aaron and Lydia to get new vegetable seeds*, she decided, *than a new cow and calf.*

Caroline held her breath and peeked outside, scanning the cabin, the yard, the garden fence, the woods. Everything seemed still. She waited. Had she imagined the intruder? No! She caught her breath as someone wearing a red shirt slipped from the trees. He appeared to be a young man, skinny and perhaps not yet full-grown. Crouched over, he darted toward the garden and disappeared behind the tall fence.

Caroline knew she didn't have much time. When the thief discovered that the loose board had been nailed down, he might reappear in the yard. Plucking up her courage, she turned to the cows. "You're coming with me," she whispered. "Garnet, I'm going to lead you into the woods. Minerva, I expect you to follow. *Hurry!*"

Garnet came along without fuss. *Thank goodness we practiced,* Caroline thought. To her relief, Minerva ambled along behind, unwilling to be separated from her calf.

Caroline led the cows out the shed door and around the corner so that the small building hid them from sight. From there, she tugged Garnet into the woods. Minerva followed, but as soon as they left the bare-earth farmyard, the cow lowered her head and began tearing at grasses with her teeth.

"No, stop!" Caroline hissed. She grabbed Minerva's halter with her free hand and tugged frantically until she managed to pull the cow's head up. With every step, Minerva tried again to snatch some fresh greens. Caroline struggled to keep her moving until they were screened behind a dense thicket. Then she gave up and rested her aching arms, letting the cow have her way.

A distant *screeech* echoed through the quiet morning. The thief had opened the garden gate! He must believe the farm was deserted. And once he'd raided the garden, he might come to steal the cows.

I need to find a better hiding place for Minerva and Garnet, Caroline thought. *But where?*

The sound of munching caught her attention. Minerva was happily eating a thick clump of plants that Caroline didn't recognize. Her heart sank. On top of everything else, the cow's milk might be ruined again . . .

Wait! Thinking of milk gave Caroline a new idea. *Maybe I can hide Minerva and Garnet in the springhouse,* she thought, feeling a flicker of hope. The springhouse was close by, but it was so overgrown with briars and vines that the thief likely didn't know it existed.

Caroline tugged Minerva's halter. The cow raised her head with a disapproving look. "I'm sorry," Caroline whispered, "but this is for your own good." Creeping through the underbrush as quietly as pos-sible, she led Minerva and Garnet to the springhouse. She managed to unbolt the door with one hand.

Minerva eyed the door and tossed her head with alarm. *Oh no,* Caroline moaned silently. If Minerva started bellowing, the thief would surely hear.

"Please, Minerva, be good!" Caroline begged in a hoarse whisper as she pulled the cow's halter again. "I'm trying to save you and your baby."

Minerva stayed quiet but tossed her head again and didn't move. Seconds ticked past. Finally Caroline let go of her halter and looked at Garnet. "Show your mama," Caroline whispered. She led Garnet, step by step, into the springhouse. Minerva hesitated, but she followed her calf. Caroline quickly shut the door behind them.

Minerva swung her head from side to side and stamped one foot. Caroline was still afraid that the cow might make a racket.

Then, as if knowing that Caroline needed help, Garnet bumped her head against Minerva to say, *I'm hungry!* The calf began to nurse. And Minerva settled down.

"Good girls," Caroline told them. "I'll be back for you as soon as I can!"

Independence Day

nce the cows were settled, Caroline slipped from the springhouse and latched the door behind her. For a moment she felt a sense of triumph. She'd hidden the cows!

But where was the thief? Was he still stuffing his pockets in the garden? Caroline didn't dare confront him. *But I should try to get a better look at him*, she thought. If she could describe the thief, Uncle Aaron might be able to catch him.

Caroline crept to the cowshed, slipped inside, and grabbed a pitchfork from among the tools hanging on one wall. She couldn't imagine using it to defend herself, but holding it made her feel braver.

Then she peeked around the door frame. Across the yard, the garden gate stood wide open. She held her breath. Had the thief already dug up all the radishes and tiny carrots and slipped back into the woods? Maybe he'd decided to raid the cabin, too. But no—as she watched, the intruder walked out through the garden gate. He wore a brown hat pulled low, and dark trousers with his red shirt.

Caroline jerked backward so that he wouldn't see her—and the pitchfork banged into a sickle hanging on the wall. It fell to the ground, clattering against a tin pail. It sounded as loud as thunder. Caroline's heart jumped to her throat as the thief froze, staring straight at her. Then he began to run.

If he'd come toward her, Caroline would have turned and raced all the way to Sackets Harbor! Instead, the thief was running away. And without giving it any thought, Caroline tightened her grip on the pitchfork and ran after him.

The thief pounded along the edge of Uncle Aaron's field. Although he had a head start, Caroline managed to gain on him. He was barefoot. Several times he seemed to step on a stone or stick and took several hops on one foot before running on.

Caroline raced after him. Her fear slid away, replaced with anger. She would scare this thief so that he'd never want to steal again!

At the back corner of the field, he turned down the path that led to the stream. Caroline had nearly caught up to him when she caught one foot on a root. She stumbled and almost fell. When she looked up again, the path ahead was empty.

Where could the thief have gone? Caroline stopped, gasping for breath, searching the underbrush for any telltale movement or flash of red cloth. Everything was still and silent. *He must be here somewhere!* she thought, bewildered.

Then she remembered the dead sycamore—the one with the hollow trunk. Holding the pitchfork firmly in both hands, she crept toward the tree. The opening faced away from her, but as she got close, she saw a pair of dirty feet poking from the hidey-hole.

She tiptoed closer, circling around the trunk. The thief was crammed inside the tree, sitting with his knees pulled up against his chest. He was younger than she'd expected—maybe twelve or fourteen. Was he a young boy from the navy who'd run away from his ship?

"Come out of there!" Caroline demanded.

After a moment, the boy crept into the open. "Don't hurt me," he begged, eyeing the pitchfork. "Please don't poke me with that!"

He looked so frightened that Caroline lowered the pitchfork. She was still angry, though. "You have no right to be sneaking about, stealing things that don't belong to you!"

The boy shoved his hands into his pockets, hunched his shoulders, and stared at his toes. "I didn't think anyone was home," he mumbled.

"That doesn't make it right!" Caroline glared at him. "Well? Why have you been stealing?"

The boy was quiet for a long moment. Then his knees seemed to buckle, and he folded to the ground. He buried his face in his hands, but not before Caroline saw tears welling in his eyes. "I'm just so *hungry*," he whispered.

Caroline's anger drained away. For the first time, she noticed how thin the boy was, and how ragged and dirty his clothes were. "What's your name?" she asked gently.

"R-Robbie," he managed, swiping at his eyes. "Robbie Parkhurst."

Caroline chewed her lower lip, wishing Uncle Aaron and Lydia were here. They weren't, though. It was up to her to handle this situation.

"Come along, Robbie," she said. She grabbed his hand and pulled him to his feet. "Let's go find you some food."

A short while later Caroline sat at the table in the cabin, watching Robbie wolf the cornmeal mush and fried fish she'd put in front of him. When he was finished, he wiped the plate with his fingers and licked them clean. "Thank you," he said. "I surely appreciate your kindness. I'll be going now." He started to rise.

"No, wait!" Caroline protested. "Please."

Robbie reluctantly dropped back down on the bench.

"Why are you so hungry?" Caroline asked. "Don't you have any parents?"

"My father was a soldier," Robbie said quietly. "He was killed in the battle at Sackets Harbor."

The grief in his eyes made Caroline's heart ache. "I'm sorry," she said. "My papa fought in that battle, and I know it was horrible. What about your mother?"

"My mama always followed the army," Robbie told her. "Me and my two little sisters, too. Mama did laundry for the men in my father's regiment, and my sisters and I did chores. In return, the army gave us blankets and a little food. But now . . ." He spread his hands, palms up. "Once Pa got killed, we had to leave the regiment."

Caroline frowned. "Why? Couldn't your mother keep washing clothes for the soldiers?"

"Army regulations say that once a woman gets widowed, she either has to marry another soldier or move on," Robbie explained. "Mama's not ready to marry again—she's brokenhearted about Pa. We've got no family anywhere near, so we just set out down the road."

Caroline couldn't imagine simply wandering, with nowhere to go. "What happened?"

Robbie shrugged sadly. "My mama hasn't been able to think straight. She's been sickly, too. When we came to an abandoned farm near here, I decided we should hole up until she got stronger and we could figure out what to do next. The cabin roof has fallen in, but there's an animal shed yet standing. We've been sleeping there. I've tried to keep us fed with wild greens and frogs and such, but I can't always find enough."

Caroline looked away. What a terrible situation!

"Please don't tell anyone," Robbie begged. "Pa would be ashamed if he could see us now."

"Were you the one who set that fishing line across the creek?" Caroline asked.

Robbie nodded. "I've never fished before, though, and I must have baited the hooks wrong. Every one was empty when I got back." He rubbed a rough spot on the table with his thumb. "It got so my sisters couldn't sleep at night. They were so hungry, they just cried. That's when I started stealing. I know it's wrong, but . . ." His voice faded away.

Caroline got up and walked to the window, trying to think. She understood that Robbie was truly desperate. Stealing *was* wrong . . . and yet if someone in her family wept from hunger, she might do the same thing.

"I'm feeling better after this fine meal," Robbie said. "I'll just go and collect my family, and we'll set off for someplace new. No one needs to know."

Caroline faced him. "I can't keep this a secret

from my Uncle Aaron and cousin Lydia. This is their farm, and you've eaten some of their food."

Robbie hung his head.

"But I'm sure they'll understand," Caroline added. She looked around the cabin. There was precious little food inside, and not much yet ripe in the garden. And she'd come here to help her relatives, not give their food away! *But Uncle Aaron trusted me enough to leave me alone today,* she thought. *I have to make the best choice I can.* And with that, she knew exactly what to do.

"We don't have much food to spare," Caroline told Robbie, "but let me see what I can find, and we'll take it to your family."

He stared at her with wide eyes. "Honest?"

"Shall we take some milk for your sisters?" she asked. "But—oh." She made a face. "It will taste like leeks."

"That's of no matter at all," Robbie assured her. He jumped to his feet, looking downright hopeful. "They'll be ever so pleased."

Caroline walked to the abandoned farm with Robbie. The small clearing was silent. Robbie led her to the rickety shed. Inside, two little girls with dirty faces and big eyes sat huddled in one corner. Mrs. Parkhurst, who looked completely done in with grief and hunger, lay on a blanket. A canvas sack hung on the wall. *That sack,* Caroline thought, *must hold everything the Parkhursts have left in the world.*

The girls scooted away when they saw Caroline follow Robbie inside. Mrs. Parkhurst tried to sit up. She looked alarmed.

"Please, don't worry," Caroline told them gently. "Robbie and I brought a little food."

Robbie set down a crock of cornmeal mush. Caroline carefully poured milk from another crock into a tin cup. She offered it to Mrs. Parkhurst, who waved a hand toward her daughters. "If you'd be so kind," she said, "please feed my girls first."

The girls drank greedily. They didn't seem to mind the flavor of wild leeks.

We considered that milk ruined, Caroline thought. She'd been worried about Lydia and Uncle Aaron having enough food. Compared to the Parkhursts, though, the Livingston family was eating very well indeed.

Caroline noticed Mrs. Parkhurst smoothing her hair as if she was uncomfortable to have a stranger see her in such a sad state. "I need to go now," Caroline told them, "but I'll be back later. I promise."

When Uncle Aaron and Lydia returned home that afternoon, Caroline told them everything that had happened. "I'm sorry I gave away food without your permission," she said. "I just couldn't bear to see anyone so hungry."

Uncle Aaron put his hands on her shoulders—just as Papa might have done when he had something important to tell her. "You did just fine today, Caroline. First you protected the cows. Then you helped a family that is truly in need. I'm proud of you."

Caroline felt a warm glow spread inside. "Thank you, Uncle Aaron."

He cocked his head toward the door. "Now, let's go fetch the Parkhursts. They can sleep snug under our roof tonight."

By the time the Parkhursts were settled into the loft in the Livingstons' cabin, darkness had cloaked the farm. Lydia and Caroline lit a lantern and walked to the cowshed to check on Minerva and Garnet. "I felt awful about spoiling Minerva's milk, but you should have seen how Robbie's sisters drank it down," Caroline said slowly. "Even though my family's been living in the middle of war in Sackets Harbor, we never had to worry about where our next meal was coming from, or where to live."

"I'll never feel sorry for myself for not having sugar again," Lydia declared. She picked up two curry brushes and handed one to Caroline.

The girls spent some time brushing the cows. Garnet pranced about for only a moment before she quieted down and let Caroline smooth her red coat. "Good girl," Caroline whispered. "Thank you for helping me today."

When she and Lydia started back to the cabin, Caroline paused to admire the stars twinkling overhead. These were the same stars she'd seen from her own home. The same stars that sailors used to help guide their ships on the great waters of Lake Ontario. Those stars reminded Caroline that she was still connected to her family, and to Sackets Harbor.

Caroline had long dreamed of sailing her own ship, letting the winds and stars help steer her course. That longing would always fill her heart. *But I will try hard not to feel homesick here, or to feel sorry for myself because I don't have a ship,* she promised herself. For someone like Robbie, her dreams would seem like luxuries indeed.

The cabin door opened. In the shadows, Caroline saw Uncle Aaron step outside and stroll across the yard to join them. "I've just had a good talk with Robbie and his mother," he told Caroline and Lydia. "I've convinced them to stay with us for a few days to gather their strength. In return, they'll help us with chores. Mrs. Parkhurst seems like a sensible woman. Once she's had a few good meals and a chance to rest, she'll be able to decide what she wants to do next."

Caroline and Lydia exchanged delighted smiles. "That's a wonderful plan!" Lydia said.

Uncle Aaron turned to Caroline. "With Mrs. Parkhurst here to help us, we can spare you for a few days. Would you like to celebrate Independence Day in Sackets Harbor?"

Caroline gasped, then threw her arms around her uncle. "Oh, *yes*! I'll come back and help here afterward, but—oh, I did *so* want to be home on Independence Day."

Uncle Aaron laughed. "And so you shall be." Then he tipped his head back and looked at the stars. "It's a fine night."

"It is," Caroline said happily. "It is indeed."

Independence Day in Sackets Harbor was everything that Caroline had hoped it would be. Townspeople and military men gathered by the harbor. Several of the officers gave rousing speeches. Caroline swelled with pride as they spoke of defending their young country.

Then every ship in the harbor fired a gun salute in honor of American independence. *Boom! Boom! Boom!* The noise shuddered over the water. Caroline gazed north, toward the British troops in Upper Canada that had twice attacked her village. *We are still Americans,* she told them silently. *We will continue to fight until you let us be!*

When the official ceremony was over, the Abbott family and their workers and friends shared a picnic at the shipyard. The men set up big tables, and the ladies set out bowls and baskets of food. The sun was hot, but a breeze ruffled the American flag flying over Abbott's. Caroline smiled as she watched these people she loved enjoy the afternoon.

She was finishing a bowl of wild strawberries served in cream—sweet cream, that didn't taste like leeks—when she heard Papa calling her.

"Yes, Papa?" Caroline put her bowl aside and hurried to join him.

"Will you walk with me?"

"Of course!" She studied his face anxiously, wondering if he had bad news to tell her, but Papa's face was calm. She took his hand.

"Close your eyes," he instructed. The corners of his mouth crinkled, as if he was trying to hide a smile. "I'll guide you."

Where was Papa taking her? Caroline felt an excited tingle as she closed her eyes and let him lead her away.

After a moment she heard the hollow sound of wood beneath her shoes. Papa had brought her onto the dock.

"You can look now," Papa said.

Caroline opened her eyes and saw a sweet little skiff sailing into the harbor, heading toward the shipyard. The sight sparked a bittersweet memory. "It looks like *Sparrow*," she said.

Papa's eyes were merry. "It *is*."

"*What?*" Caroline squinted toward the skiff. It did look just like *Sparrow*. Mr. Tate was sailing the skiff. As it drew closer, he dropped the sail so that he could row to the dock.

Caroline turned to her father with astonishment. "But—but I sank *Sparrow* in Hickory Creek weeks ago! I *ruined* her!"

"Not quite ruined," her father said. "Ever since you told me what happened, I've wanted to raise the skiff so I could see if the damage could be repaired. I knew it would please you."

A lump rose in Caroline's throat. With all that Papa had to worry about, all he had to do, he'd thought about raising the skiff? To please *her*?

"That morning when Aaron's letter arrived," Papa

continued, "I *knew* you didn't want to leave home. Yet you went without complaint. It helped me realize how much you've grown up since the war began."

Caroline opened her mouth, then closed it again. She couldn't find words.

"So Mr. Tate and I salvaged the skiff. As it turned out, the damage was easy to repair." Papa's voice was full of mischief. "And once the woodwork was sound, I decided the skiff needed a new name." He pointed.

The skiff had almost reached the dock. Grinning, Mr. Tate used the oars to turn the boat broadside. Caroline gasped when she saw the new name spelled out in fresh blue paint: *Miss Caroline.*

"Would you like to go for a sail?" Papa asked.

Caroline clapped her hands. "Oh, *yes*!"

Soon she and Papa were settled into the skiff. Their friends and family waved from the dock. As Papa rowed through the harbor, a military band on shore struck up a tune. The crisp rattle of drums and the clear tones of bugles drifted over the water. It was fine music for Independence Day, both fierce and lively.

The skiff sailed out of the harbor and into the open water of Lake Ontario. Waves danced blue and green into the distance. Caroline laughed for the pure joy of it all. "Shall I raise the sail?" she asked.

"You're the captain," Papa told her.

Within minutes, Caroline had set the sail. *Snap!* The wind caught the canvas. *Miss Caroline* skimmed over the water. A gull called as it glided overhead.

Caroline felt her spirits rise even higher, and soar toward the horizon.

INSIDE Caroline's World

People who visit the peaceful village of Sackets Harbor today might find it hard to believe that in Caroline's time, a fierce battle took place there. On May 28, 1813, the British sent warships across Lake Ontario to capture Sackets Harbor and destroy *General Pike*, a powerful warship being built there. The British knew that few American soldiers were on hand that day to defend the village.

But the Americans had luck—and nature—on their side. Before the British ships could reach the harbor, the wind died. The ships were stalled offshore, giving townspeople and farmers time to prepare to fight. The wind finally picked up at dawn on May 29, and the battle began. Just as the sun was rising, nearly 900 British soldiers landed west of town.

Abbott's Shipyard and the events that take place there are fictional, but the other details of the battle are true. The fighting went on for hours. When it seemed that the British were about to win, American soldiers set fire to their own storehouses so that the enemy could not capture valuable supplies. At just about the same time, though, the British gave up. The burning storehouses were lost, but the Americans had won the battle.

Soon after, *General Pike* was completed. The great warship patrolled Lake Ontario for the rest of the war, and Sackets Harbor was never attacked again.

Other cities weren't so lucky. On August 24, 1814,

the British invaded Washington, D.C. They burned the White House and left much of the city in ashes. Thanks to the bravery of First Lady Dolley Madison, however, important treasures were saved from the White House.

Three weeks later, the British attacked Fort McHenry, near Baltimore. The battle raged all night, but as the sun rose, an observer named Francis Scott Key saw the American flag still flying. Overjoyed, he wrote "The Star-Spangled Banner," which became the national anthem.

In December 1814, Britain and America agreed to end the war. But news traveled slowly by ship across the Atlantic Ocean, so word didn't reach America for nearly two months. In the meantime, British and American soldiers fought one more big battle, the Battle of New Orleans. It was a resounding American victory. Because of that, many Americans felt their country had won the war. But some experts say neither side won. Thousands were killed, and many civilians, like the Parkhursts, suffered greatly. Neither side gained even an inch of land.

Still, by winning several key battles against the British—the strongest fighting force in the world—the United States proved that it was a nation on the rise and its independence had to be respected.

After the war, the United States stopped trying to expand into Canada. Instead, settlers focused on pushing west. Like Caroline's Uncle Aaron, they carved farms out of the forest and built roads and towns on the frontier, changing America's landscape and boundaries forever.

Read more of CAROLINE'S stories,

available from booksellers and at *americangirl.com*

⤳ *Classics* ⤨

Caroline's classic series, now in two volumes:

Volume 1:
Captain of the Ship
When war breaks out and
Papa is captured, Caroline
must learn to steer a steady
course without him.

Volume 2:
Facing the Enemy
The war comes closer and
closer to Sackets Harbor. Can
Caroline make the right decision when the enemy attacks?

⤳ *Journey in Time* ⤨

Travel back in time—and spend a day with Caroline.

Catch the Wind
Go sailing with Caroline, help raiders capture an enemy fort,
or ride an American warship to a hidden bay! Choose your
own path through this multiple-ending story.

⤳ *Mysteries* ⤨

More thrilling adventures with Caroline!

Traitor in the Shipyard
Caroline suspects one of Papa's trusted workers is an enemy spy.

The Traveler's Tricks
Caroline and Rhonda ride a stagecoach—right into trouble!

≥ A Sneak Peek at ≤

Catch the Wind

My Journey with Caroline

Meet Caroline and take an unforgettable journey
in a book that lets *you* decide what happens.

I run outside, slamming the door behind me. Now that I've left the air-conditioning, the air slaps my skin like a hot, damp towel. I run across the lawn and plunge down the path that leads through the woods to the pond.

This has always been my special place. It's shady here, and quiet. I plop down on the grassy bank, bring my knees up, bury my face in my arms, and cry.

I haven't cried this hard since I was little. As little as the twins, maybe. Thinking of them makes me angry all over again. I haven't heard Mom tell *them* that they have to do extra chores while she's away serving on a navy ship. I haven't heard Dad tell *them* that they have to be extra brave. It's not fair.

After a while I run out of tears. I raise my head and wipe my eyes. My breath is all shuddery and my nose is running.

"Would you like a tissue?" Mom asks quietly. I hadn't heard her following me, but now she sits down on the bank too. I wipe my eyes and blow my nose. "I'm sorry this is so hard on you," she says.

"Ple-e-e-ease don't go away!" I beg. "I want you to stay home with us!"

Mom's mouth twists sideways like it does when she's thinking. Finally she says, "Sometimes it helps to talk. Can you tell me what you're afraid of?"

I've never told Mom that I'm afraid, but she's smart about guessing stuff. I'm bursting to say, *"Everything!"* I have to clench my teeth to hold that word inside.

It's true, though. I'm afraid I won't have time to do *anything* except help Dad with the twins while Mom's gone. Even worse, I'm afraid I'll miss Mom so much that I'll be miserable every single second of every single day. I'm afraid that Mom will get hurt. Worst of all is imagining her sailing away. Those navy ships are huge, but still puny compared to all the water in an ocean.

Mom gently brushes my hair from my forehead. "I don't *want* to be away from my family for so long, you know," she says. "I'll miss you every single minute."

"Really?" I ask.

"Really," Mom says. "But I'm also proud to serve my country. My father served in the navy, and his father before him. It's a chain of service that hasn't been broken for over two hundred years! I want to carry on that tradition. And I want to make the world a safer place for you and your sisters," she adds quietly.

"I need you to be brave. Can you do that for me?"

I am positive that I won't be able to do that. I wish I *were* brave, like Mom. But I'm not.

Mom says, "I want to give you something." She holds out her hand with fingers curled over the gift.

She's got a present for me? I hadn't expected that, and I feel a teensy bit better. Mom and Dad have promised that I can get my ears pierced on my next birthday. Maybe she picked out special earrings for me!

What she gives me isn't a little jewelry box, though. Instead, my present is round and hard and made of metal. A piece of glass protects a dial on one side.

I glance at Mom. "Um . . . is it a pocket watch?"

"No," Mom says. "Take a closer look."

There are only a few letters on the dial: N, NE, E, SE, S, SW, W, NW. Now I get it. "You're giving me a compass?" I ask, totally confused. What's the point in having a compass when you can use GPS?

"I'm giving you a very old compass," Mom explains. "My father gave it to me when he was shipping out for a voyage at sea. He got it from his father, and so on. This compass goes back to the very first person in our family to serve in the navy. That was during the War of 1812."

I can tell that Mom thinks I should be excited about this, but honestly, I wish a pair of sparkly earrings had gotten passed down in my family instead.

Mom gives me her *This is important* look. "Sailors in our family have always used this compass to navigate. I hope it will help remind you to steer a steady course while I'm at sea." She closes my fingers over the compass. Then she gets up, kisses the top of my head, and starts walking back to the house.

After a moment I lie down and wriggle to the edge of the bank. I see my reflection in the still pond below. My eyes are all red and funny-looking from crying.

I hold the compass in front of me. The gold part is dull and dented, and the glass is cloudy. What am I supposed to do with it?

I turn the compass in my hand, but the needle on the dial keeps pointing in the same direction—north. Right now, it's pointed straight at me. The needle looks like a little arrow aimed at my heart. I think about how Mom going away *feels* like an arrow in my heart.

Suddenly I see movement in the water below. My reflection is trembling, as if someone had tossed a rock into the pond. The water ripples and sloshes until my face becomes a blur. Feeling dizzy, I close my eyes, the compass clutched tight in my hand.

After a moment the dizziness passes. I open my eyes. The water is still, and I can see my reflection again.

Except . . . it's not me.

I blink. The face I see in the water is mine, but I'm wearing an old-fashioned bonnet. This morning I put on a bright red T-shirt with sequins, but now I seem to be wearing something pale blue with white lace around the collar. And instead of the pond's muddy bottom, I see stones through clear sparkling water.

That's so spooky that I scramble to my feet, almost tripping because that pale blue top I saw reflected is actually a long dress.

Gulping, I look around. The summer heat is familiar, but that's all. Instead of the little pond, I'm beside a humongous lake that stretches away into the distance.

What is going on? I feel dizzy all over again.

"Are you looking for warships too?"

I whirl around. A blonde girl about my age is walking toward me, easily making her way over the stones. She's wearing a long pink dress and looks as if she belongs in a play or something.

I open my mouth, then close it again. Finally I stammer, "Did—did you say *warships*?"

The girl looks out over the lake and clenches her fists. "They're out there," she says. She looks half angry and half scared. "We drove them off yesterday, but they'll be back."

I don't like the sound of *that*. "Um . . . who, exactly?"

"The British, of course!" she exclaims. "Those black-hearted British will repair their ships and sail back across Lake Ontario again."

Back to *where*? "This might sound stupid," I say, "but can you tell me where we are, exactly?"

She looks startled. "Why . . . you've reached Sackets Harbor, New York. The village is just around the curve of the bluff." She grins, and now the worry is gone from her face. "My name is Caroline Abbott. Who are you?"

Her smile is so nice that I can't help smiling back, as if we're sure to become friends. I introduce myself. "And I just arrived," I add, to help explain why I have absolutely *no* idea what's going on.

"So you don't know about yesterday's battle," Caroline says. "British ships formed a line in front of Sackets Harbor and fired cannonballs at us! It lasted for hours."

My jaw drops. Have I really and truly landed in the middle of a war? *Oh, Mom,* I think, *I wish you'd stayed with me back there by our pond!*

"But our gun crew fired back," Caroline's saying proudly. "And I helped!" Since she's just a kid, I can't imagine how she was able to help a gun crew. Before I can find out she asks, "Have you traveled far?"

That almost makes me laugh, even though it isn't funny. "Yes," I say again. "Very, very far."

"Are you traveling by yourself?" She looks behind me, as if expecting someone else to appear.

I look around too. We're standing on a narrow strip of stony shore. A rough rock wall, all drippy with moss and ferns, rises straight up behind us. No one else is in sight. "Yes," I tell her. "I'm alone. And I guess I . . . well, I sort of got lost."

"Now that war has been declared," Caroline says, "lots and lots of people are traveling to Sackets Harbor." She sighs. "I think eighteen-twelve is going to be a very difficult year."

Eighteen-twelve? I seem to have traveled over two hundred years back in time!

About the Author

KATHLEEN ERNST grew up in
Baltimore, Maryland—not too far from
the place where, during the War of 1812,
Francis Scott Key wrote the United States'
national anthem, "The Star-Spangled
Banner." While writing about Caroline,
Ms. Ernst had a wonderful time exploring
Sackets Harbor, New York, and the
Kingston area in Canada. She lives in
Wisconsin with her husband and cat.